WITH MY WHOLE HEART

With My Whole Heart, Book One

I0525756

MariaLisa deMora

Edited by Hot Tree Editing

Cover designed by Debera Kuntz

First Published 2017

ISBN 13: 978-0-9983267-6-4

DEDICATION

To those readers who make a point to be always
present in my life: Thank you. A special
thanks to Lu Bielefeld, for inspiring this story
with a well-placed word.

CONTENTS

ACKNOWLEDGMENTS

Happiness isn't always about getting what you want. Sometimes it's about putting other people's happiness first. That's how you build a sustainable bank of happiness, because increasing the quotient you have is directly related to what you hand out to the ones you love.

Here's to those brilliantly generous people who help make so many dreams surrounding family come true. The selfless donors, carriers, and surrogates. The couples and single parents who want a life for their children beyond what they can provide. The doctors and nurses who care and nurture, who encourage and weep along with their patients with every setback and success. You are all amazing, and your roles are so very important.

Quick shout out to Brett. He took the time out of a busy schedule to set me straight on what a high school basketball coach would, and would not, do. Any errors are my own and persisted despite his guidance. Thanks, my man, very helpful!

Thanks, as always, to the beautiful Becky Johnson and her folks at Hot Tree Editing. They take my words and shine them like a diamond. Thanks also to my alpha team: MirandaPanda, Jamey, Jesse, Kori, Kelsi, and Megan. Candor is a good thing! Thanks for putting up with me. Thanks also to Debera Kuntz, for creating the cover of this book from words on thin air. Your work is fabulous, as are you my dear!

Sometimes all it takes is a well-placed word to spur the creative process. The idea for this story was planted by a Brazilian fan and blogger who posted a review for a story she didn't enjoy. I immediately followed the well-worn 'what if' path, and within about fifteen minutes had sketched an outline for the story.

I was in the middle of working on another book and couldn't begin writing this one right away. Fortunately, good things come to those who wait, right? Once I'd settled my schedule so I could pay attention to the characters, I found this story that wouldn't leave me alone required in-depth research as I knew nothing about the world of surrogates. I hope I got it right, but any mistakes are mine alone, and not the fault of the individuals and professionals I spoke to on the topic.

After several weeks of research, I pulled my laptop close and began writing a story that flowed so very well, it felt like silk in my head. It is absolutely amazing when that happens, and what you hold is the result. I truly hope you enjoy Jaime and Connor's story.

Woofully yours,
~ML

Chapter One
Jaime

Jaime rested her chin on the backs of her curled knuckles, staring down at the newspaper-covered table in front of her. She shifted and reached out, picking up a pencil and putting an X on the last viable help-wanted ad. Twenty-eight circles of lip-chewing hope turned into twenty-eight crossed-off dead ends. She cut her gaze to one side, eyeing her phone. No need to use any of the limited data left on her pay-by-the-month plan, she knew the balance in her checking account to the penny. *Not nearly enough of those to go around*, she thought, turning back to the paper and scanning the rest of the ads, hoping she'd missed *the one* that would lead to a job.

"Mom!" The shout came before her son even had the door open, his hands and body hitting it at a run, as was usual for Nathan. "I'm home." There was nothing

1

quiet about Nate. The door slammed closed behind him, and his quick footsteps echoed through their tiny apartment. He was always excited to see her, excited to get home; Nate was just excited about everything. *Please God, let him keep that same attitude through life*.

"In here," she called and twisted in the chair, opening her arms. Two heartbeats later, Nate barreled through the hallway and ran to her. At nine, even with his abilities, or maybe because of them, he hadn't yet learned that hugging his mom wasn't cool, and she wrapped her arms around him as he snuggled into her shoulder. "Missed you, handsome. You have a good day at school?"

Muffled against her shirt, he said, "Yeah. Missed you too, Mom."

A year ago it was still Mommy, she thought, giving him a tight squeeze before she let him go. So much change in a year. *For the better*, she promised herself.

"Any luck?" He'd pulled back a couple of inches and was eyeballing the table.

Jaime blew a quick raspberry against his neck, and once he was giggling, she admitted the truth. "Nope. Not today. There's always tomorrow, though."

With eyes older than his years, he stilled, staring at her for a moment, and she saw when he consciously decided to ask the question he more often avoided. *Another clue that my baby's growing up*. "Do we have enough for the apartment?" He paused, then pushed a little further into territory that was uncomfortable for them both. "What if you can't find a job, Mom?"

"I will have enough," she promised, and it wasn't a lie. Tomorrow she'd go to the plasma donation center. It would be her sixth visit, which all their paperwork said would give her a bonus big enough to pay rent with. She could use the ATM in the center's building to check the balance of her card when she was done, make sure they kept their promises. "And I'm gonna find a job. It's just taking longer than I thought it would."

"Because of me." Nate's nose wrinkled and his chin quivered. "Because I can't stay after school anymore."

Crap. Time to lie.

"The afterschool program wasn't working out anyway, honey. I didn't like the guy in charge any more than you did. I didn't like him at all." Nate had gotten into a fight last week when one of the older boys was picking on a girl. "And you did the right thing, making sure you took care of Jacqueline." The girl was a little older than Nate and had Downs Syndrome. The boy had been goading and insulting her, trying to make her cry. "The way you stepped in when you did, it kept her from getting her feelings hurt. I told you then, and I'll tell you now, I'm proud of you, Nathan Grimes. Doesn't matter what Mr. Watts said." Watts was the program organizer and a sleazeball of the highest order. Jaime'd had to dodge a come-on from him a dozen times in the month and a half that Nate had been going to the afternoon program. "Jacqueline's mom said you were brave and didn't back down." Nate hadn't been the first to throw a punch; that had been the twelve-year-old boy. Program rules were clear, though, and both parties had been suspended for a week. Then Jaime's temporary assignment had ended, and she didn't need the child care. "Plus, your time in the pokey is up, so if I needed you to go, the door would be open again. All you'd have to do is apologize to the boy."

Nate shook his head. "Like I said when Mr. Watts told me to the first time, he should have to apologize to Jacqueline. Not until that happens, Mom. It's not fair."

"I don't disagree, Nate. But that's not the rule." He pulled away in frustration, slinging his backpack to the floor beside the couch with more effort than was necessary. "I don't want to argue, and we don't have to, because you won't be going back for a while. Not until I find a job." He wrinkled his nose at her again. "Stop it, worrywart. It'll all work out. Now, pull your homework out while I get you a snack. Tell me what you have to do."

Rolling his eyes, Nate turned to his backpack, pulling out a fistful of papers. "I have to make a model of a cell."

In front of the refrigerator, Jaime paused and looked back, not sure she'd heard him correctly. "A jail cell? What kind of class is that?"

Laughing, Nate turned to her, and she caught her breath at the sight of him. Nate might have her hair and eyes, bright blond and a brilliant, clear blue, but the deep dimples embedded in each cheek were his father, all over again. *God, I miss you, Brice.*

"No, Mom. You're goofy. It's for science." Shaking his head, Nate picked through the papers and plucked one out. "The structure of a cell nucleus. You know, sciency stuff. The nuclear envelope, nucleoplasm, chromatin, endoplasmic reticulum, stuff like that." He looked at the table. "Can I use part of the newspaper, Mom? Oh, and, do we have flour? If we have some, I can use that and a little salt to make the model." Glancing at her, he frowned. "Fridge door is open, Mom."

Closing the door with a bump of her hip, she stared at him in amazement. Not for the first time, either, because Nate was gifted. "Where did you get those brains, boy? We need to return them, ASAP. You sure didn't get them from me."

He grinned again and then ruined the effect by rolling his eyes. "These are my brains, Mom. You've lived with me long enough. Should know my brains from some stranger's brains by now." Tipping his head to the side, seeing far too much in her expression, he quietly asked, "Are you okay?"

Yeah, I'm okay. I'm just scared out of my mind. Because you're so smart, so very smart, and I'm afraid I can't do right by you. I'm scared because I'm alone and I don't know if I'm doing the right thing, so I question myself about a thousand times a day. I'm sad because your daddy died, and his parents hate me, and so they hate you, too. And I hate them for taking that away from you. For making it so you don't have anyone to take to school on Grandparents' Day. For making it so you only have me at your back. Because, what if I mess up? I'm so scared that I'm going to mess up, mess you up, and you're so smart and good.

She didn't say any of that. Jaime would keep the smile plastered on her face until she died before Nate learned what was inside her head. Instead, she told him, "Yeah, I'm just trying to figure out how I'd know if you had some stolen brains in your head." Holding out the snack cup, she said, "Applesauce first. I'll round up the ingredients for whatever crazy concoction you're intending to make." She grabbed a spoon from the drawer and held that out, too. "What did you need again?"

"Salt, not a lot, and flour, about three cups." He took them from her hands and turned to the table. "Plaster of paris, Mom. Easy stuff."

"So you say." Turning to the cabinets, she was in the process of dragging everything out when there was a loud knock on the front door. "You stay." She looked at Nate then pointed to the bag of flour, setting a plastic measuring cup next to it. "The stuff is all here, but wait for me."

Looking through the peephole, she froze for a minute, running the date through her head to make sure she hadn't missed the deadline by mistake. No, the rent wasn't due for two days, so why was the apartment manager at her door? She put the chain on, then unlocked the deadbolt, opening the door the three inches allowed by the chain. "Mr. Solon, what can I do for you?"

He was so close to the door all she could see was one eye, but from her view of that limited part of his face, she could still see he was glaring at her. He'd clearly heard the chain going on, and decided to be annoyed she'd take that precaution against him. "Got someone interested in the apartment. Need to know if you're going to stay."

"Yes." She wanted to follow that with something else, something profane, but held her tongue. In the months she and Nate had lived here, she'd been late with her rent twice, but managed to pay the money within the Tennessee-mandated fourteen days, which meant Solon hadn't been able to evict her. It didn't stop him from threatening her with it, though. And surely didn't stop him from harassing her, like this.

"I plan to be in and out of the apartment, showing it." He lifted his lip in what resembled a smile. A near copy, but not a good one. "You know, just in case."

"Mr. Solon, if I'm not here, the lease doesn't allow for your presence in my apartment without agreement." She paused, liking the flinch he showed her, but knowing she'd pay for it sooner or later. "I don't agree." *Take that.*

"You're pushin' it, Grimes." The corners of his mouth turned down, and he pulled back several inches, both eyes boring into her. "Get your rent to me on time this month."

"Was that all, Solon?" She could match his unpleasantness, and would. He nodded, and she closed the door, flipping the deadbolt, not caring if he heard it.

Turning around, she gasped and clutched at her shirt, startled because Nate stood directly behind her. "What in the world?"

"He stopped me in the lobby." Nate's eyes burned blue, anger shining through. "Told me he hoped you were home. Hoped he wouldn't have to call CPS on you leaving me alone. I told him you were here, Mom. I'm sorry."

"Don't worry, honey. He's a little man with a tiny bit of power, makes him think he's a big deal." She shook her head. "Applesauce?"

"All gone. I need a big bowl for the plaster." Nate's eyes slid from her to the door. Then he stepped around her and turned the thumb lock on the knob with a decisive motion. His protectiveness reminded her of his father, and she loved seeing that part of Brice come out in their son. "I'm ready to get started, Mom. If I turn it in this week, I get extra credit." He grinned at her.

"Since when does fourth grade science give extra credit?" Jaime rocked back and forth on her feet, smiling down at Nate.

"Since I'm taking ninth grade science." Shaking his head, Nate laughed, which had been her goal. Back in the kitchen, she took her largest mixing bowl down from the cabinet and placed it on the counter.

The principal of his school had called her in at the beginning of the year to talk about the standardized placement test results. Since Nate had been in a different school each year, sometimes twice in a year, no one but she had really understood just how smart he was. Until now.

"Miss Grimes, Nathan is reading at a high school senior level, and on his own has demonstrated his capability to solve pre-algebra and pre-calculus math problems. I can't place him in the classes he needs. Not officially, not without the district doing their own testing, but I can tell you that he will be bored with fourth grade classwork." Mr. Paterson, the principal, had looked so stern and serious it had taken Jaime a minute to realize Nate wasn't in trouble. Once she caught up, she realized this was a discussion about how well he was doing and nothing negative.

"I'd like to challenge him, and keep him focused on academics that will stretch his mind and intellect. At minimum, Nathan should audit the science and math classes for eighth and ninth grades. I can promise you that I'll expedite the district testing and will personally oversee his instruction until we have a ruling." When Jaime didn't respond, Paterson finally cracked the somber expression he'd been wearing, evidently reading she was still nervous about the entire conversation. *"This is a good thing, Miss Grimes. An exciting thing. We don't want him to slip through the cracks. Nathan is extremely intelligent."* He leaned forwards, emphasizing the word as he repeated it, *"Extremely."*

"Well then." Jaime shook herself, walking back towards the chair where she'd been seated. "You better get to work, since it's ninth grade science and all." She

9

picked up the rest of the newspaper and settled back in to read.

Reclining in the huge chairs reserved for the donors, Jaime stared at the ceiling as she counted to sixty, then squeezed the ball. *Last one*, she thought, and relaxed her hand, letting the ball rest in her palm.

"Okay," she heard, and turned to face Trisha, her favorite tech. "Lemme get this spun out, and we'll load you back up." Trisha disconnected the bag and held it up in front of the scanner on the wall. It flashed amber, then green, and Trisha turned to smile at Jaime. "Don't forget to check your balance. It said you reached the bonus."

"That's good." Jaime released a relieved sigh, smiling back at Trisha who was now frowning.

"You need the money that bad, honey?" Jaime was the only client in the center right now, and the rest of the techs were in the break room where there was juice and fresh fruit, which meant she and Trisha had some privacy. "You okay?"

"Jobs are few and far between these days." Jaime shrugged and sighed again. "What you have in your hand is my rent money for this month."

Trisha made a face as she worked with the bag and machinery, then leaned on the countertop while they waited for the plasma to separate from the cells that would be returned to Jaime's body. Head tipped to one side, Trisha asked, "You have a little boy, right? Nate?"

Jaime nodded, knowing she was smiling. "Any trouble with the pregnancy?"

Shaking her head, Jaime snorted a laugh. "Unbelievably easy. Pregnancy seemed to suit me. From the moment I knew I was pregnant, I'd never felt better. I had morning sickness, but only for a couple of weeks. After that, smooth sailing."

Still serious, Trisha asked, "You liked being pregnant?"

"Yeah, what's not to like? Knowing you're cradling and nurturing new life? I loved it." Jaime lifted the hand that wasn't tied to the arm of the chair, holding her palm up at Trisha. "Not saying the delivery wasn't hard, but even that wasn't as bad as everybody made it out to be." She considered the look on Trisha's face and dropped her hand back to her belly. "Are you preggers?"

"Me?" Trisha laughed, reaching out to flip a switch on the machine, removing the bag to finish the process. "No way. I have no desire to be a baby maker." She cut her gaze to Jaime, then back to the bag. "But my cousin's girlfriend's sister did this pregnancy thing. Paid decent money. She was able to keep working, too."

"A surrogate?" Jaime frowned. "Is that even legal in Tennessee?"

"Yeah, totally legal. They had a contract and everything." Trisha reattached the bag, hanging it on the pole next to the chair. "There we go, honey. Almost done."

Jaime stopped at the library on the way home. Using the computers in the lab there, she pulled up the apartment website and clicked the button to pay her rent. Within three minutes the cash card the donation center used to transfer funds was almost completely empty, but she and Nate were guaranteed a roof over their heads for another month. She glanced at the clock, saw she still had thirty minutes before Nate would be home from school, and on impulse, opened a browser to a search engine.

Fifteen minutes later she walked out the front door of the library, two dollars' worth of printouts in her hand, head spinning from her hurried research into contracted gestational carriers and surrogacy.

"Mom." Nate's complaining tone finally registered, and Jaime looked up from the closely-printed text on the paper she held in her hand. "You're not even listening to me."

"Sure, I am, buddy." When he scowled at her, she grinned and admitted, "Well, I am now, anyway. What's up?"

"I have to paint the model." He gestured to the plaster half circle he'd crafted from covering bits of newspaper with the flour and salt concoction the night before. "I asked if you had any food coloring." She shook her head, and he grimaced, then she could tell he was thinking hard. "Markers. There're old markers in the kitchen drawer." He rushed that direction, then yelled over his shoulder, "I need five or six little jars. Do we have anything like that?" He was digging in the junk drawer now, pulling out the old markers that Jaime had intended to throw away weeks ago. "Pliers!" he shouted happily, and turned to give her the double-dimple grin, the one she'd do anything for. The sight of that got her up and moving.

Squatting in front of the bottom cabinet, she moved a pile of pots and brought out a box, taking six small glass jars from inside. "If baby food jars will work, then we're covered. How are you making paint?"

"Scissors!" This shout was as happy as the previous one, and he ran to the table, grabbing the leftover newspaper from the previous night. "The markers are dry, but they have ink inside still. I just need to use primary colors so I can make strong paint fairly quickly. I'll crack the tubes open, cut up the marker bits and put just a tiny bit of water on them in the jars."

"How do you know how to do this?" Jaime shook her head. "I get it, and I see how it will work, but how did you think of it?"

"I dunno. How do people think about anything?" Nonchalant about his idea, after spreading the newspaper on the floor, he got to work, both hands on the pliers as he opened one of the tubes.

"You need my help, Nate?" It was clear he didn't, not really, and that felt strange. *Where did my little boy go?* "Let me cut up the marker tips. Those are sharp scissors."

Without speaking, he nudged the scissors in her direction, then using the pliers, held up a long, red piece of what looked like felt. "Pink, red, and a little purple can all go in the same jar." She stood and grabbed the tongs she used to serve food, and then took the marker tip from him. Nate grinned at her, then bent his head back to his self-appointed project. Soon they had tidy piles of the remains from dismantled marker tubes on one side, and a line of glass jars with color-sorted marker tip bits that were slowly marinating in water. "Makin' marker juice, Momma. Good job." She laughed, reaching out to ruffle his hair, stopping when he said, "I saw Mr. Solon today. He said the rent is paid."

Jaime pulled in a breath, shaking her head at how the manager seemed willing to use her child to leverage against her. *Asshole.* "Yup, we're good to go for a while."

Nate touched the inside of her elbow with one finger, gently tracing along the edge of the bandage that covered the skin there. "You okay, Mom?"

Jaime leaned down and pressed her lips to the top of his head, tears stinging her eyes. "Right as rain, Nater Potater. Right as rain." She swallowed hard. "I love you a lot, you know that?"

"I love you, too." His voice soft, Nate returned the words to her. They were quiet for a minute, and Jaime tried to etch this moment on her memories. *He's growing up so fast.* Nate cleared his throat, then said, "I'll let the markers sit for a bit, then finish the model."

Chapter Two
Connor

"Good hustle." He lifted the whistle to his lips and blew hard, creating a piercing sound that echoed through the gym. The squeaking slide of shoe soles on varnished wood stopped and one of his seniors cradled the ball on his hip. Thirteen pairs of teenaged eyes locked on him as he walked out from the sidelines. Connor held up his hands in a wordless request, catching the ball when it was thrown. "Good hustle," he repeated, "but we're trying to play pack-line defense and keep the ball out of the paint. You—" He pointed at one of the kids, then tossed the ball. "—are over there gambling on every pass that comes your way. Need to be a team player to be on a team." Two quick blows of the whistle and he said, "Reset and run it again" and walked back to the sidelines.

"Coach," he heard, and looked over his shoulder at the kid he'd reprimanded. A sophomore, he'd been a stud on the court back in junior high, but now was one of a handful of talented players at the high school level looking to make a name for themselves. Connor could almost predict the next words.

"I can't play that way."

Nailed it, he thought, and held up a hand to stop the forward from beginning the play. "Can't doesn't belong on my court." Connor shook his head. "Can't is for people who want things handed to them. Who don't want to work for them. Can't is for kids who don't have discipline and drive. Can and will? Those are for players, men and women who aren't afraid of a little hard work. Can you?" Connor tipped his head at the scoreboard which would show the score if this was a game. "Board will tell. Will you?" Connor lifted his chin and looked the kid up and down, watching as the boy's own chin came up to match his posture, how his shoulders squared up. "I think you will. Now let's play ball."

When practice was over, Connor made his way to the office adjacent to the gym, going through his e-mail that had come in over the afternoon. He printed out several, packed them into a folder and had just stood, finger to the switch of the light he used on his desk when Jordan Bates, one of his senior boys came to the doorway.

"Coach?" Connor gave him a level gaze and waited. "Can I talk about my grades? I suck at chemistry, and I'm afraid I'm gonna fail."

Shit. The school had a no pass, no play rule like nearly all academic institutions, and this was never a good start to a conversation. Beyond basketball, the kids needed a solid educational career so they could get into a decent college, and move on from here. He tossed the folder down on the desk and rolled his chair out to sit, "Sure, son. Tell me what's going on."

Two hours later they'd hammered out a strategy to help Jordan keep his science grade up, and Connor had praised him for coming forward before things had become unrecoverable. He turned off the light and picked up the folder, locking the door behind him as he followed the kid out into the hallway. "You got a ride home?"

"Yeah, Coach. I'm covered." The kid started trotting away, and then turned, running backwards. "Coach Con, you're the best."

"Yeah, yeah. Just bring the attitude you have on the court to the books. Make it worth my time." Connor laughed and pushed through the door to the parking lot.

Home or diner? He started the truck and sat a minute, folder on the seat beside him. *I go home, I won't eat*. The rumble from his stomach settled things, and he pulled out, headed towards a nearby twenty-four-hour diner.

He ordered his usual without referring to the menu, and then pulled the papers from the folder, taking a pen from his shirt pocket. He was digging through the stack, making notes as he went along, things he needed to handle or respond to, and items to research. This cut down on his time in front of the computer, and he found he'd do nearly anything to make that happen.

The waitress appeared at his elbow, plates in hand. He shifted things to accommodate the dishes, putting the stack of papers he had finished back into the folder, leaving just a few on the table. "You're always working when you come in here," the waitress said, and he looked up, seeing a coy smile on her face. "You ever just have some fun?" Hands on her hips, she waited for his response.

"I have fun all the time." He unwrapped his silverware, smoothing the paper napkin across one thigh.

"You ever wanna have fun with me?" She dipped her chin, looking at him from underneath her lashes. "I could give you my number."

"I think I'm all booked up for fun, sorry." Connor kept the smile on his face, hoping the fact he wanted her out of his space didn't show. "Thanks."

With narrowed eyes, she stared at him for a minute, then pulled his ticket from the pocket of her apron. Turning to walk away, she tossed a clear understanding of where they stood over her shoulder. "Let me know if you need anything."

Chapter Three
Jaime

"Hi," Jaime said, keeping the slight smile on her face. "I'm interested in the surrogacy fertility program you have. How can I make an appointment to meet with someone to discuss it?" She let the smile drop and shook her head. Taking a deep breath, she began again, her expression serious. "Hi, I'm Jaime Grimes. I'm interested in applying for the surrogacy program your clinic offers. Can I make an appointment to talk to someone?"

The mirror Jaime stared back at her, clear blue eyes locked on hers. "I can do this."

One bus transfer later, Jaime stood in front of the clinic, staring up at the sign over the doors. "Am I really going to do this?"

In her mind, she pictured Nate's face, imagined having the money to pay for the classes she knew he would need. Imagined not having to worry about rent. Imagined having breathing space for a few weeks or months. Then she imagined seeing the faces of the parents who would love and cherish a child, seeing it as a gift of life. She remembered how she felt when she carried Nate, the sense of rightness and joy she had.

"I'm going to do this."

Chapter Four

"We have all your test results back, Jaime, and I'm pleased to tell you that everything looks great. Your history is perfect, the previous uncomplicated pregnancy and birth are good indicators that you're a physical candidate. Your psychological workup is really good, too. The notes say that you liked being pregnant, and you're looking at this as a chance to give someone a family. That's exactly what we want in a gestational carrier or surrogate." Sarah, the case worker assigned to Jaime, smiled broadly at her. They'd first met on the day Jaime walked into the clinic, nearly two months ago.

Jaime smiled back, pulling her purse closer to her body. *If everything is so wonderful*, she thought, *then why does this feel like a rejection?* "That's all good, right?"

"Right. That is all very good. I do"—Sarah slipped a paper from the folder on the desk in front of her, and lined the edges up neatly—"have a few additional questions about your family."

"My family? I don't see them much. My brother is in San Diego. My mom and dad are divorced. She's in Oregon, and he's in Florida. About as far apart as they could get geographically and still stay in the states." Jaime laughed nervously.

"Do you know of any major illnesses or diseases?" Jaime shook her head, and Sarah made a note. "Your grandparents?"

"Not that I know of. My mom's parents were killed in a boating accident. I was about ten, I think. Daddy's parents are both dead, but they lived well into their eighties." Jaime smiled. "We're embarrassingly healthy."

Sarah rested her hands on the paper and looked at Jaime for a minute. "Okay." She smiled. "We're done with this part. Now, comes the tough stuff." When Jaime lifted an eyebrow, Sarah laughed softly, shaking her head. "Matching you to prospective parents. Since you're willing to go either the surrogate or carrier route, that opens the playing field quite a bit, and we've already tentatively matched you to several profiles based on your evaluation." Sarah picked up the folder and handed it to Jaime. "Here are the profiles of interested couples that I'd like you to review."

"Wow, so fast?" Jaime was taken aback, and knew her face showed her unease. "I expected it to take a while."

Sarah spoke soothingly, her confidence helping Jaime come to terms with what had been said so far. "Not fast, we've been working towards this for a few weeks now. Jaime, you're an optimal candidate in a high-demand situation. Take a couple of days and look through the profiles, see what you think. The fee structure is different for each, but don't let that be your deciding factor. Each profile is in the forty to sixty thousand range. If there is one in there that you are interested in pursuing, I'm certain I'll hear from you quickly."

Sarah stood, and Jaime did as well, her breath coming quickly. It was the first time she had heard the dollar amounts and believed they were real.

"When you leave my office, go directly to the clinic downstairs. They'll be expecting you. We'll go ahead and do a quick test so we can see where we are in the cycle. You can pick up your prescription for prenatal vitamins at the same time." Walking around the desk, Sarah held out her hand, and Jaime tried not to clasp on too tightly. "You're doing a very good thing, Jaime. A special thing. Thank you."

Seated on the bus headed back to the apartment, Jaime held the folder against her chest, arms folded defensively across it the whole way. She knew there wouldn't be any personal information in the profiles, nothing to identify the individuals; still she wanted to keep them safe. Felt a responsibility to these potential parents to make sure they were protected.

In the door, she slipped off her shoes, lining them up neatly to the side and wandered into the kitchenette, placing the folder on the table.

She looked around, taking inventory of where she and Nate lived, the first time she'd allowed herself to do this in a while. It was a small, single-bedroom apartment. Furnished, the couch was a foldout, but she didn't bother most of the time, so her sheets and blanket were stacked neatly at one end, wedged in along the arm. The kitchen and dining area were a tiny space, carved off the end of the living room. There was a small table and two chairs, but it was just her and Nate, so no need for anything more. The way the building was laid out, their apartment was surrounded on five sides by their neighbors. Sounds of arguments and fights, babies crying, and occasionally a dog barking could be heard all day long. At night, there would be the loud noises from TVs. Those never-ending sounds she tried to ignore from the news, and movies, and games, or more shouting.

What would it be like to give Nate more? Give him what he needs? Jaime filled a mug with water from the tap and put it in the microwave, waiting the sixty seconds the old unit needed to heat the water enough for tea. *At forty, I could move us to a better apartment. Get him in good classes. Put money away for his college.* Moving by rote, she opened the cabinet and pulled down the tin of tea. Opening a bag, she stuffed the wrapper into the tiny trash can kept under the sink, and dunked the bag into the mug. *At sixty thousand, I could buy a house. We don't need much.* She looked around. *We've never needed much.*

Carrying her mug of tea, she walked to the table and sat in a chair. Pulling the stiff cardboard towards her, Jaime took a deep breath and flipped it open.

Jaime clutched the phone, wrapping the cord around her wrist and turning so her voice would project into the waist-high booth. The library was quiet, even here in the basement where the kids' section was. Nate was at one of the tables, books spread in a semicircle around him, more comfortable here where the furniture was right-sized than he was upstairs. When he needed to study, she helped him lug the books back and forth, and would run interference with the volunteers if they didn't know him. The library kept a row of phones for local calls down here, to help people do their job searches.

"This is Sarah."

Startled, because it was Saturday so she'd been expecting voice mail, Jaime stumbled over her own greeting.

"Hey, Sarah. Hi. This is...um, Jaime." She paused, not sure what she should say next. Fortunately, Sarah didn't have any problems.

"Jaime, hello. I'm so glad to hear from you. Have you had a chance to go through the profiles yet?"

Glancing over to Nate, Jaime verified he was still engrossed in his work. He was busy researching a paper on cell mitosis, which was more extra credit. "Uh, yeah. I did. There were more than I expected."

"If there aren't any profiles in that group that are of interest, then I have several other couples who have already reached out." Papers rustled in the background, and she imagined Sarah flipping through more prospective parent matches.

"No. I mean, yes. There were two profiles that jumped out at me." Jaime tipped her chin down, studying the scuffed toes of her shoes. "Two couples."

"What are the identification numbers? I can pull them up and answer any questions you might have." Sarah sounded so certain, so sure of herself. Jaime glanced at Nate again and caught him looking at her.

"I don't have that with me. The folder I mean. It's at home. But I had a question." She didn't want to turn her back on Nate, but also didn't want him to overhear her. Reaching up, she cupped her hand over the speaker, hoping to stay quiet enough that he couldn't hear. "The couples? It doesn't say gender? On the profile?" She knew she sounded like a hick, ending every sentence with an uptick in her voice like it was a question, but she couldn't help it. "You know? What gender they are?"

"No, the profiles don't have that information. We like to match people without making sexual orientation a big deal. If you have issues with gay or lesbian couples, you should have mentioned that before, Jaime." Now Sarah sounded disappointed, and Jaime rushed to reassure her.

"No, I don't have any problems with gays. I just wondered. It would be...my brother is gay. He and his partner haven't talked about children, not with me or the family, but I know they'd need to do this, or adoption. I thought it would be kind of paying it forward if one of these couples were gay." Jaime chewed on the inside of her cheek, waiting for Sarah's response. She hadn't put her brother's sexual orientation down on any of the answers, but none of the questions had come straight out and asked.

"I think that's admirable, Jaime." Sarah's voice was soft, like she was touched by what Jaime had said. "All the right reasons. Do you remember anything about the two profiles? I could try to look them up."

"I'll go over them again when I get home. The next step is the interview, right? So, either way, if they don't like me, or if I don't like them, we can go back to the list?" Jaime knew this already, but she wanted confirmation that nothing had changed.

"Exactly right, Jaime. We do a video interview, so it's low pressure on both sides. Give me a call as soon as you're ready to do that. We'll get moving and start the process. I'm glad you called. I'm always willing to answer whatever questions you have." Sarah paused, then said, "Goodbye, Jaime."

"Bye, Sarah." Carefully, noting her hand shook, Jaime put the handset back into its cradle. She was still for a moment, staring down, thinking about the impact this one decision would have on so many lives. Her and Nate, the parents, the child. A touch on her hip, so familiar she didn't even have to look around to know it was Nate. "Yeah, honey?"

"Who was that?" Jaime twisted her neck, looking at him. "On the phone just now, who did you call?"

Crap. She wasn't ready to talk about this with anyone yet, not just yet, and the first person would not be her nine-year-old son. "A lady who is helping me with something." Jaime glanced at the table, seeing the books now tidily stacked to one side. "Did you get finished, or just need more books?"

"I'm finished. What's she helping you with?" Nate's eyes didn't waver. He stared at her with an intensity that was nearly frightening.

Direct was probably the best idea right now, so she asked, "What do you want to know, Nate? What are you asking about?"

"Are you sick?" Jaime watched as Nate's lips flattened, and his jaw got tight. *Crap.* This was something he seriously worried about.

"No, I'm not sick." *At least that's true*, she thought. "Why do you think so?"

"Because you don't eat much, and you had blood tests, and then I saw an envelope you left on the counter. It was from a clinic, Mom." Pulling in a breath, he leaned against her side, ducking his chin. "I don't want you to lie to me. If you're sick, just tell me."

"Nate. No, honey." She squatted, putting one knee on the floor. "I'm not sick. I don't eat much because I'm not hungry much." *Okay, that's a lie. But, hopefully he won't call me on it.* "I donated plasma again. That's the bandage you saw on my arm. And the envelope from the clinic was to give me good results on a couple of tests they ran. Good results, honey. Nothing bad. I promise."

"Why'd they run tests if you aren't sick?" Nate avoided looking into her face until she reached out, cupping his chin in her palm. "Clinics don't just run tests, Mom."

"You're right," she said, and shook her head. "I'm kind of applying for a job. They needed to make sure I wasn't sick and didn't know it. So they did some testing. The envelope you saw was the results, which were all good, Nate. Nothing bad, honey. I just didn't want to say anything until I know for sure if I can do the job or not." She paused, and he stared at her, expression serious. "I promise you, once I find out for certain, you'll be one of the first people I tell."

"Okay." Nate nodded, and her hand moved with his chin. He kept his eyes locked to hers, and said, "I'm glad." He squinted, and she realized it was to try and hold back tears when he said, "I was worried."

"I see that now, Nate. I'm sorry you worried. You should always, always ask me when you aren't sure about something. That's the only way we can make sure we stay on the same page." She squeezed his chin, and then moved her hand to rest on his shoulder. "We're a team, right?"

"Yes, ma'am. We sure are." One corner of his mouth curled up, and he asked, "Can you help me carry the books back up? I'm ready to go."

"You betcha," she returned, standing. Ruffling his hair with her fingertips, she told him, "Let's get this done and we can catch the bus. Get our behinds home faster. I'm thinkin' waffles tonight."

"Waffles are good." Back at the table, he piled the lion's share of books into one stack and wrapped his arms around it, lifting the heavy burden with a grunt. "If you—" He hefted the books a little, adjusting his grip. "—can carry those—" Nate jerked his chin towards the three books left on the table, and finished, "I can get these."

Jaime waited for him to turn away before letting her grin escape. *My little man.*

Can't put it off any longer, she thought, nervously smoothing her damp palms down her pants. "It's not like they can see me. They can't see me looking at their information. Can't see me making a decision." Taking a deep breath, she picked up the folder and walked to the kitchenette, pulling out a chair. Standing for a moment, she laid the folder on the table, and then sat down in a rush, her bottom thumping solidly on the seat. "I've already looked through them. I'm not sure why this is so different." Jaime rolled her eyes and shook her head. "Annnnd, I'm talking to myself."

Glancing over, she made sure that Nate's door was closed, then lay one palm flat on the folder. *Let me make the right choice*, she prayed, and opened the folder. At the top of the pile were the two profiles that had drawn her interest the first time she went through the paperwork.

She took her time, reading through each piece of information. Both couples had compelling stories, written to engage the prospective carrier or surrogate, but Jaime found herself circling back to the same one, again and again. A couple looking for an egg donor also willing to be the surrogate.

Loving. Caring. Stable relationship. Supportive family and friends. Successful professional and a stay-at-home parent with a five-year-old child from a previous surrogate arrangement, wanting to add to their family unit. As impersonal as the description was, the language made her believe that this was something this couple wanted very much. They'd been down this road before, finding a match only to have it fall apart, and eventually getting the baby they desired. Now, knowing the ropes, they were tackling the system again, hoping against hope to bring another baby home.

She read it again.

Loving. Caring.

They knew the odds, knew the cost and risks, and still were willing to brave the stream.

This is it. She lay the paper on top of the pile and gently closed the folder. *This is right*.

Next morning, after getting Nate to school, she transferred busses with the folder in hand and continued on, arriving at the clinic just as they opened. The receptionist smiled at Jaime and waved her up to the window as she worked the lock to slide it open. Jaime told her, "I don't have an appointment or anything, but I wanted to leave a note for Sarah."

"You found a good match?" The woman reached for the folder and plucked it from Jaime's suddenly numb fingers. "This one?" Lifting the top sheet of paper free, she lay it to the side, looking at the identification number in the top corner. "Let me just take a peek." Fingers moving over the keyboard, she pulled up information on her computer screen, comparing it to the profile sheet. "Oh, perfect. They have not yet been matched." Picking up the phone, she dialed and then spoke, "Jaime Grimes is here. She's interested in the..." She lowered her voice so Jaime couldn't make out the words. A moment later she nodded, then said, "I'll send her right back." Fingers to the button underneath the counter, she pointed at the now-unlocked door with her other hand.

Seated in the chair beside Sarah's desk moments later, Jaime watched as the printer spat out paper after paper, forms and releases that Sarah had her sign. Grinning at Jaime, Sarah said, "This is nearly my favorite part. Introducing you to the parents." Leaning back, she turned the screen around so Jaime could see the pictures. "Next to watching them take their baby home, that's my favorite."

Jaime had stopped listening, gaze locked on the screen as she scanned the features of the couple in the picture gallery. The woman was blond, nearly as blond as

Jaime, with light-colored eyes, while the man had dark hair and eyes. They were nearly the same height; he was slightly taller than his wife when they were standing side-by-side, and in front of them was a gorgeous little boy with dark hair. He looked so much like the man it had to be his son.

Sarah had kept talking, and Jaime tried to tune back in on what she was saying, not making sense out of the words for a moment. "...accident, and for her it is medical, so they need both donors. The intent was to have the same donors as last time, but the egg donor who helped with little Samuel is no longer available. We still have access to the sperm donor so the children will be half-siblings, biologically. Your physical makeup is exactly what they hoped to find. They've already greenlighted you in the hopes you'd select their profile, so they are ready to meet you as soon as you can."

"That's not his child?" Jaime flicked her glance at Sarah, then back at the screen. "What happened?" She shook her head, wishing she could take back the question. "Never mind, it doesn't matter. They look so happy, and the little boy looks like him, that's all. So they want to do a video chat soon?"

"They'd actually like to meet you, but we'll begin with a video, yes. Jaime, I've been working with you for nearly two months, and you've been able to clearly articulate your thoughts on being a carrier or surrogate. I don't have any hesitation letting you meet them. For most of the parents, they've been through so much, we don't allow contact until after all the contracts are filed and we've started the first cycle. I just won't put them through more heartache." Sarah tipped her head to the side, smiling softly. "For you, the only concern I still have is that you haven't talked about telling your son yet, and we'll want to make sure he understands what this means. Nine is an impressionable age, so we'll want him to understand that Mom's not giving away his little brother or sister."

Jaime grinned at her knees. "Nate is not like that. He's..." She lifted her eyes and looked Sarah in the face, trying to find language to explain without raising more questions. "...very mature for his age. I will talk to him soon. It just didn't feel really real before now." She gazed at the pictures on the screen showing the little family standing, then sitting in a grinning group at a picnic table, an image of the mom in a kitchen, one showing the dad riding a bike, and a final one of their little boy climbing on a backyard jungle gym. "It's real now."

Jaime and Sarah were moving to a small conference room when Sarah got called away for something in the office. She pointed to the door and turned away, leaving Jaime to go in by herself. Inside was a table with a half dozen chairs and a phone, while against the wall was a large screen. Jaime sat in one of the chairs and leaned forwards, palms resting lightly on her thighs. Blinking fast, she was near tears, thinking about those pictures. Imagining that could be Jacob and Trent with a child. *It's a good thing*, she told herself again, and laughed, because she honestly didn't need any more reassurance. Seeing the faces had made it real. The device on the table beeped, lights flashing red and green, and on the screen she saw a notice that said, "Calling." Pulling the round speaker towards her, she accidently brushed the button to accept the call, and then the video resolved to a view of a kitchen.

No one was in frame, but off screen she heard a woman ask, "Do I look all right, Cooper? I'm so nervous. Why am I so nervous to meet her?"

A man's voice answered, laughter in his tone, "You look perfect, Marie. Pretty as a picture. I promise you, this momma is gonna love you."

They're talking about me, she marveled, realizing they were as anxious as she was. The door opened and Sarah bustled through, calling out, "Perfect, we're already connected. Ready to go, Thompsons?"

"I am," Cooper called, and Marie laughed when he said, "Marie's a little camera shy today."

Then Jaime was staring at the screen as a widely smiling woman came into view, her husband's hand on her hip. She and Marie could have been sisters. *Wow*, she thought.

"Wow," Marie said, her voice breathy, and Jaime laughed.

"I was just thinking that." And with that, the ice was broken, and Jaime found herself in a friendly if inquisitive conversation without any awkward silences, where the back and forth was effortless. It felt real and right, and that was what she told the couple just before Sarah disconnected. "This feels right."

Marie reached over and laid her hand on Cooper's arm, and he covered her fingers with his own hand. "It really does. I can't wait to meet you, Jaime. We'll see you Monday."

"See you Monday."

The screen went dark, but Jaime didn't turn. After a few moments, Sarah laughed and said from the door as she pulled it closed behind her, "I'll give you a minute."

Cooper had a bike accident that rendered him infertile. That was when he was in his early twenties, just before he had married Marie. Marie had polycystic ovarian syndrome, and had undergone many rounds of unsuccessful treatments to try and conceive, and then carry a baby. Finally, nearly seven years ago, they had started down the path of surrogacy. The story Marie told was practiced and polished, but the pain they'd suffered to build their family was plain. Two matches that fell through before they found an egg donor and a gestational carrier that they were comfortable with. The sperm came from Cooper's brother, which explained the familial resemblance. Instead of looking for another egg donor, the current plan was to use one of Jaime's eggs.

Is this the right thing to do?

The black screen didn't give her any answers.

It feels right.

At some point this had gone beyond Jaime thinking about the money, and now it was a chance to help Cooper and Marie create the family they deserved.

Chapter Five

This would be her third phone call of the morning, and Jaime was anticipating making this one with excitement rather than trepidation. Explaining the process to her mom and dad had gone well, once they got over the initial shock of her announcement. Fortunately, both had accepted her reasons at face value, not digging any deeper.

She knew the conversation with Jacob would go a bit differently. She also knew he would get it, every aspect of her decision, and prayed he would support her. She didn't have any reason to think differently. He had always been the one guy she could count on. Leaning against the tiny kitchen table, she waited for the ringing phone call to connect.

"My baby sister! Is everything okay?" Hearing Jacob's voice always made her smile.

"Everything is perfect. I just wanted to call and chat." That alone would be enough to tell him it was an important conversation, because she never just called and chatted unless it was the end of the month and she had a bunch of minutes left.

"Okaay." He dragged out the word, making every sound a communication of caution. *Yup, he picked up on that.* "What do you wanna chat about?" He sounded reserved, and she cast her mind back to the last time she'd heard this tone from him. It had been right after Brice died, when she'd been struggling with everything. A single soon-to-be mother who had lost the love of her life. If he were flashing back to those days, it was no wonder he was treading carefully. "James, you sure everything is okay? Is Nate okay?"

"Nate is perfect." She rushed to reassure him, hoping the smile on her face sounded in her voice. *I love that nickname.* "The school is so good for him, Jakey, you'd love it. He loves it, and the classes are pushing him. In a good way, you know? It's crazy to see my fourth grader lugging around a high school English composition book. Crazier still to see him working on extra credit stuff, just because he's so excited about whatever it is they're studying. I don't understand half of it, but I don't have to. He's got more in his head than I'll ever have. God, I'm so proud of him." She pushed off the table and walked to the couch, sitting on the middle cushion so she could swing her legs up and lie back, relaxing into the soft furniture with a sigh. "See, things are good."

"Then what do you wanna chat about?" He revised his previous question, and she grinned at his persistence. *That's my Jakey.*

"Have you and Trent ever considered expanding your family?" Trent was Jacob's long-term partner, his husband. They'd been together as a committed couple since before Nate was born. Jaime loved Trent like a brother and loved how her brother was with him.

"Yeah, but the cost is crazy. Adoption has become easier for gays over the past few years, but still invites a level of scrutiny that Trent and I are just not comfortable with." He made a noise, sounding frustrated. "There're surrogates, of course. But then we hear stories about how the process is so iffy, with women changing their minds and keeping the baby. I have at least three friends who had that happen. Broke their hearts. They were there for the sonograms and heard the heartbeats and everything. So hard to watch people dealing with that kind of thing. Puts me off the idea, ya know?" He sounded sorrowful, sad, and she hated that for him.

"But you know about the process of surrogates and stuff?" She shifted, shoving a throw pillow underneath her head. *Time for the hard part.*

"Yeah, we've looked at it, even talked to a couple of registries and agencies. We're…just not ready to follow through. Not yet. Maybe someday." He chuckled. "Trent as a momma, I'd love to see that." With a sigh, he asked, "Why all the questions, James?"

"I'm going to be a surrogate."

Silence greeted her announcement, stretching on so long that she squeezed her eyes closed, waiting for him to unload on her with whatever was going through his head. Then he shocked her, tears thick in his voice when he said, "That's amazing, Jaime Raquel. Absolutely...amazing is the only word I have. What a gift. A precious, precious gift."

Now Jaime was the one who couldn't speak, and she sniffed, wiping her nose on the back of her wrist. Through a clogged throat, she whispered, "It ain't rocket science. But it's something I can do."

She could almost see Jacob settling onto the sectional in his living room with a mug of hot tea, questions bubbling over as he sorted through the details with her, proving once again that her big brother was the best sounding board and friend she could hope to have. At the end of the conversation, she felt even more determined to help Marie and Cooper. When Jacob finally hung up, she stared unseeing at the door, her vision turned inward where she again saw the joy on the couple's faces. "I'm going to make a baby."

"Nate, when you're finished with homework, I'd like to chat." Jaime rinsed the last plate, stacking it in the dish drainer as she scooped up the clean silverware, running it under the hot water before stuffing it into the little cup she had taped in the corner of the drainer. She ran the wet rag over all the countertops in the kitchen, finishing with the faucet and edges of the sink. After wringing it out, she draped the cloth over the top of the faucet and turned, dishtowel in hand, wiping water from her fingers while she watched Nate at the kitchen table.

He was working his way through a complicated math problem, and even with him being engrossed, she knew he'd heard her, so there was no need to demand a response. While she waited, she moved to sit on the couch with her book, reading about the manner of romance in regency England. Absorbed by the story, she didn't notice when Nate finished, just complained when he intentionally jostled her as he joined her on the couch. "Hey."

"We talkin', Mom?" He bounced on the cushion again, and Jaime was reminded that he was only nine years old, not a teen yet, and playtime always needed to be on his schedule. The challenge was other kids, because the ones his age weren't engaging to talk to, and the ones who could hold a conversation with Nate were driving and dating. *Ugh.*

"Yup. I want to talk about something I'm considering." *Doing*, her brain supplied, and she winced. He stilled, glancing at the front door, and then back to her. *Odd.* "You know about babies." He narrowed his eyes, squinting as he nodded. "Yeah, not my favorite conversation, either. But bear with me, buddy." He wrinkled his nose and angled his chin down, keeping his eyes on the cushion between them. "Some people, some women and men, have trouble having babies." She'd already thought through this, knowing he would appreciate the scientific details, but wanted to get to the meat of the conversation before he got distracted. "Or they're like your Uncle Jake, and can't have babies. Not without help. So when that happens, they have a couple of options."

She paused, and Nate filled in one of the blanks, like she expected him to do. He had two friends who were adopted, and their parents didn't make a big deal out of it, but didn't hide it either. "Adoption is one way."

"Right. Exactly right. There are a lot of babies out there who need homes, but sometimes that process, the adoption piece, isn't right for the couple." She took a moment to compose herself and pulled in a breath. "Those couples do something called surrogacy, where they make an arrangement with a woman to help them have a baby. Not an easy thing, and there's lots of technical stuff that I can tell you, but I wanted you to know I've decided to try and help a couple have a baby." He opened his mouth, and she rushed to finish before he interrupted. "I've talked to them, and I like them. They are super nice. They've already done this once, and have a little boy. He's four years younger than you are. But they want to have another baby. And that's where I come in." She paused now, to give him a chance to break in with questions but he just stared at her. "If it all works the way the doctors say it will, then I'll carry a child for them, and once that baby is born, it will be entirely theirs. Not ours. Does that make sense?"

Raising his chin, he looked at her. "We're studying reproductive cells." He stared intently, wanting something from her, but she didn't have enough clues yet to know what. "In science, I mean. I know how the zygote is made, how the embryo starts. It's a sperm and an egg. How..." Nate's voice faltered, then he picked up the question, never looking away. "How do the sperm and egg work with this?"

Not the question I expected. "Well, the egg will be from me. The doctor will take it out, and put it in a laboratory, and then they'll have the sperm and introduce it into the same—" *Don't say test tube, that sounds weird.* "—container." She held his gaze, giving him time to ask whatever else he wanted.

"And then?" His nose wrinkled again, but he never looked away, even though his fingers were working nervously along the seam of his shorts. "What happens then, Mom?"

"And then they put it back inside me. And nine months later, their baby will be born." She sighed in relief when he dropped his eyes, glad he'd accepted the brief explanation.

"And you'll be okay?" His fingertips plucked and pulled at a loose thread. "You'll be...okay?"

"They've been doing these procedures for a long time now, and it's all safe, honey." He darted a glance at her face, then back down. "I'll have the normal baby stuff. Some tummy troubles at first, and then lots of doctor visits as we go along. Nothing's going to happen to me." Jaime studied him and reminded herself again that he was only nine. "Want a hug?" He didn't answer, just threw himself at her. Jaime pulled him into her lap, letting his head rest above her heart, bending her neck to nuzzle into his hair. "I love you, Nathan."

"I love you, too, Mom." He sighed. "Are they nice?"

"Very nice. So very nice, and they want to have a baby so much. It's a blessing to be able to do this for them, honey." She squeezed him, tightening her arms around him. "They know about you, know I have a little boy, but I haven't told them much about you, yet. If there was one thing you'd want them to know, what would it be?"

"Don't tell 'em about the school stuff." That was an immediate response, and his rejection of something so core to who he was surprised her. "Don't, because then if the baby wasn't like that, they'd be disappointed."

"Hmm. Okay, so the big brain piece is a no-go." He giggled, and she squeezed him again. "If not the big brain, then what?"

"Tell 'em I like to ride bicycles. And I'm good at basketball. And I do my homework without being asked." He lifted his head, looking up into her face with an unsure grin. "And that I hate broccoli and love pork chops."

"All good things to know," she agreed. "I'll share those with them when I meet them next week. Do you have any other questions?"

"About a million." Still grinning, Nate tried to arch one eyebrow like his favorite superhero character often did. He failed, as usual, and they laughed when both of them rose nearly to his hairline. "But I can wait."

"Meaning you're going to do your own research." He nodded, and she smiled, relieved the conversation had gone so well. "Okay by me. Less talking I have to do."

"Mom?" In the process of crawling out of her lap, Nate paused and looked up at her again. "You'll be okay, right?"

"Yes, I will." First him worried she was ill, and now this. There seemed to be a deeper reason for his concern, but she would wait to try and dig it out later. "I promise."

Chapter Six

"You're going to have to get out of the car, ma'am." The cab driver's voice surprised her, and Jaime whipped her head around, staring at the man who was scowling at her. "I got another fare."

Scrambling towards the door, Jaime tugged on the handle. "I'm so sorry. I just got distracted." She'd already paid him, and once she was on the curb with the door closed, the vehicle pulled out into the circular drive, headed towards the quiet street that led out of the development. Turning back to the house, Jaime's head tipped back as she stared up at the columns and sweeping porch. *It's a beautiful house. Made for a family.*

Swallowing hard, she took a step up the walkway as the front door opened. Marie came through and stood on the edge of the porch, hands out in welcome. "Jaime," she cried as her face lit with a broad smile. "I'm so glad to finally meet you."

Two additional video interviews and one contract later, their futures were now connected in a way that Jaime still had trouble wrapping her head around. Not that she'd had any misgivings about the process, but the fact that this woman would be caring for and loving a child they would work together to make. It still was surreal that they looked so much like the other. Like sisters.

She walked up the handful of stairs to place her hands in the offered grip, taking comfort from the fact Marie's hands were as cold as hers. The two women stood and stared at the other for a moment, and Jaime saw a matching welling of tears in Marie's eyes. "I'm a hugger," Jaime blurted and felt Marie's fingers convulse around hers. "Can I...would you mind if I hugged you?"

Marie didn't answer with words, but she pulled Jaime in close and released her hands, lifting her arms and wrapping them around Jaime. Returning the embrace, she felt Marie shift, felt a pressure on her shoulder as Marie rested her head there. "I'm a hugger, too." The words were whispered, accompanied by a sniff that made Jaime smile. "I'd love a hug," Marie said belatedly, and Jaime felt a squeeze.

"I'm glad," she whispered the words in response. "I'm so glad you're a hugger."

"Marie, is she here? Is Jaime here?" A masculine voice came from the still-open door, and the two women pulled back slightly, turning to look. Jaime watched as the good-looking man she'd seen on video came through the door. Cooper smiled and extended a hand with a

47

smile. "I see she is. Hello, Jaime. Is Marie already all up in your space?"

His words worked to break the tension and Jaime laughed, her palm meeting his in a quick shake. "I think I was the one in her space first." She glanced at the woman. "I was so nervous, but she put me right at ease."

Marie's arm wrapped around her waist and she urged her towards the door. "Let's head to the kitchen. I've made a light lunch for us. I was too nervous to eat breakfast, so now I'm starved."

Inside, Marie and Cooper led the way, and Jaime looked around curiously. Huge rooms with high ceilings, the living room and den were both filled with comfortable-looking, overstuffed furniture that invited you to sit and stay a spell. The walls were what held Jaime's attention, and few other details registered as she looked at the pictures that decorated the rooms.

Not too many so it felt crowded, but they were grouped in ways that told the story of the people in the images. Here were pictures of a much younger Marie and Cooper, together and separately surrounded by smiling people who looked enough like them so you knew they were family. Marie's group was smaller, her parents and an older couple certain to be grandparents. Small, but you could tell at a glance they loved one another.

Cooper's was more expansive, and in more than one image he stood with arms over the shoulders of two men who looked to be slightly younger versions of him. His brothers, the twins Cole and Connor. His parents were with them in one picture, then the boys, their mom, and an older woman, a huge, white farmhouse in the background. That was probably after his grandfather had died, leaving the farm to his only daughter's husband, Cooper's dad. Jaime had learned that about Cooper from the background dossier provided. He'd been eighteen and in school in New England, withdrawing to come home and take care of family. Cooper had transferred to a local college, not letting anything stop him from following his dream while making certain the people he loved were okay.

She drifted along the wall to where another group of frames were hung. These were from the couple's wedding, and many of the same faces were smiling in these images, too. There was only one brother standing with him here, though, the second twin serving in the military at the time. Jaime let her gaze travel to the fireplace mantle and saw the polished wooden frame there, a triangle holding the flag that had covered that brother's casket. Cole. *Tragic*, she thought, her gaze glancing back across all the pictures of the three boys together. They'd clearly been close, like her and Jacob.

Then came the pictures of Marie, Cooper, and Samuel, and Jaime was surprised to see a woman in some of them. She didn't look like either of them, and Marie decided she must be either Samuel's egg donor or the gestational carrier. It made her throat tight to think about them maintaining a connection with the woman after Sam was born. Connor was in the pictures, too, and it was clear he had a close relationship with his nephew.

She realized that Marie and Cooper had paused, waiting for her to finish her scan of the pictures. "You have a beautiful family." She looked back at the flag, knowing the loss it signified. Cole, dead before he really had a chance to live. *Like Brice*. Tipping her chin away from the couple, she swallowed hard. "I'm so sorry for your loss. It's so hard to see promise like that cut short. So young. Before they have a chance to fly."

"He loved serving his country. Born to it. Some men are. Cole struggled in school." Cooper's voice didn't hold any sorrow, and Jaime turned to look at him, seeing he was looking up at one of the pictures on the wall of the three brothers, a look of pride on his face. "The army gave him a purpose. He didn't like being away and missing things, like me marrying this beautiful woman." His arm tightened around Marie, pulling her against him tighter. "But he loved serving. If he had to go, he at least went doing something he loved." His gaze turned to Jaime, and she saw the loss in his smile, but his expression was also filled with love. "Let's get something to eat. And if you have any pictures of your family you'd like to share, we would be honored to see them."

"I'm so glad you chose me." Jaime felt her eyes grow round and she ducked her chin, horrified her mouth had just blurted those words. That fear fell away when Marie laughed. Jaime raised her gaze to see a broad smile on her face.

"I like to think that we chose each other." She held out a hand, "Now come on, and let's go sit down."

Connor

Standing just around the corner from the living room, Connor was glad no one had heard him come in the front door.

Marie and Cooper both knew where he stood on this meeting, and it wasn't in favor of it at all. If they'd seen him, they would have clammed up, afraid to set him off. He was excited about them having another baby, knew it was something Marie had dreamed of nearly since Sam was put in her arms.

With a gestational carrier, he had no worries there. There was absolutely nothing to tie the baby back to the womb that nurtured during the pregnancy. Needing an egg donor, well, he got that it took two to tango, and with Marie's eggs not an option, a donor was necessary. But he'd urged them to do a blind donation, not someone you had to look in the face for nine months. Sperm donor, also a necessity, and one he was honored his brother had asked him to do again.

Connor didn't get confused, though, didn't have any issues with Sam calling him Uncle Con. Never thought of the boy as his child. Sam was Cooper's kid, end of story. This, though? Having the egg donor and carrier in one person and then getting to know that person intimately? Mistake.

That was how he'd felt until five minutes ago, at least.

51

Hearing this woman express sorrow at the death of someone she never knew shocked him, but her sincerity couldn't be questioned. She sounded like she knew how it felt, and the genuine sadness in her voice picked at the scar he carried inside him.

When Cole had died, he'd known it. The minute it happened, he'd felt it. That damn psychic tie so many twins had that he and science couldn't explain. The echo that had been so strong between them, always. Bicycle wrecks and broken hearts, everything had been shared between the two of them.

It meant the very instant his brother was no longer breathing on this earth had branded in his brain. Connor had been on the basketball court, taking a class of freshmen through a new set of drills when it felt like his heart exploded. He'd fallen to his knees, hands clutching his chest, silent in the face of an overwhelming pain. Scared the fuck out of the kids. They'd thought Coach was having a heart attack, and two of them had dialed 911, calling the sheriff to the school before he could stop them, leaving Connor to have to try and explain something he couldn't even put words to.

Four days later, when the same sheriff came visiting they'd shared a knowing look. It wasn't news to Connor that Cole was gone. Not to him. The silence in his head was enough proof for him.

If I'd gone in the military with him, I would have been there. Could have saved him. That was the only thing he and his twin had ever really argued about, and in the end,

Cole's driven need to protect and serve had won out, separating the two men for the first time in their lives.

Connor hadn't felt the same calling, though. Cole had enlisted and headed to boot camp, and Connor had gone to college instead.

He listened to the murmur of voices grow softer, more distant and knew Cooper, Marie, and the woman had gone into the kitchen. Connor had been supposed to meet her, not understanding why Cooper wanted him to have a face to go with the carrier's name, Jaime Grimes, but he'd been willing to go along with it. He'd laughed and told his brother, "Least I can do."

Connor lifted a hand, knuckles grinding roughly across his sternum, accepting the pain as his due.

Knowing this woman standing in his big brother's kitchen understood about loss, too, he couldn't go in there. Couldn't face her, afraid she'd see the guilt he tried to keep buried. *If I'd been there.*

Turning on his heel, he stalked to the door and went out, closing it soundlessly behind him.

Jaime

Marie glanced up at the clock over the stove and then back to Cooper. She appeared to be studying him, undecided about something. Jaime set her empty glass on the table, the rattle of ice cubes bringing Marie's attention to her. "I'm so glad you invited me today." That wasn't a lie, either, because getting to know the couple had made Jaime even more determined to make this happen for them. "I need to call a cab, and then I'll be out of your hair." She smiled and reached across the table, covering Marie's hand with her own. "So very glad." She squeezed then released, pulling her phone from her back pocket.

"Let me get you more tea." Marie's offer came quickly, and she was up and out of her chair before Jaime could respond.

Cooper intervened, his voice quiet when he said, "Marie. Jaime's got to go." He twisted his neck and smiled at Jaime. "Nate'll be home soon. And we"—he turned his smile on his wife—"need to pick up Sam from daycare."

Marie turned around, and her scrunched-up nose looked so much like an expression Nate used that Jaime had to stifle a laugh. "Connor didn't come."

"You knew it was iffy." Cooper shook his head. "He probably had to work. It's middle of the week. He probably had trouble getting a substitute."

Call made, Jaime put her phone up and asked, "Substitute?" She knew a lot about Marie and Cooper, but Connor was more of a mystery.

"He's a teacher," Marie said, at the same time Cooper said, "He's a coach." He laughed, walking to his wife to clasp her hand in his. "He's both, actually. Teaches history and coaches basketball, too. Always been a multitasker."

"That's nice." She tried to keep the frown from her face when she asked, "He was supposed to come today? I didn't know." *Good thing, too. I was nervous enough about meeting Marie and Cooper without knowing I was to meet the entire Thompson clan.*

"He's worried." Marie leaned against her husband. "With Sam, the donor and carrier weren't the same person. He's been concerned about our choice this go around. I wanted to set his mind at ease, and I knew just from the videos that meeting you would be what he needed." She shook her head. "He worries."

Jaime thought about Jacob and Trent, and knew if they were starting this process, she'd be worried too. "I understand." She smiled. "If I get a chance to meet him, I hope I can reassure him. I'm not surprised he's concerned. I know from experience how brothers can be like that."

A horn sounded from the front of the house, and Jaime stood, patting her pockets to make certain she had everything. "Thank you again. I'm so glad to meet you both. I'm ready to get started as soon as the clinic calls."

Marie pulled away from Cooper and came to Jaime, wrapping her arms around her tightly. "We're going to make a baby," she whispered in Jaime's ear.

"We are."

"We're late, Nate" she called, digging through the pockets of the jacket Nate had thrown on the couch. "Get a move on, Grimes. Put some hustle in your bustle."

"Minute." He sounded distracted, so as soon as she retrieved the item she was looking for, she went to the doorway of his room. Tongue trapped between his teeth, he was seated on the edge of his mattress, bent nearly double as he scribbled in a notebook.

When he didn't look up, she reminded him, "We're late. You don't want to be late for the first practice." He jerked his gaze to her, then back to the notebook with a nod. She smiled as she shook her head, having seen him like this more than once. Caught up in an idea, he could be lost in his head within moments, and stay that way for hours as he wrote and researched to prove or disprove his theory. "Wanna stay home?" Without looking up again, he shook his head. Fingers tight around the pen, his hand flew across the page for another few seconds. Then he folded it neatly and tucked it into the book open on the bed in front of him.

"Ready," he said. He looked at her, but she knew from his expression he didn't see her face. Whatever this was, it had a tight hold on him. He didn't move, didn't rise from the bed as she waited, giving him a minute to pull himself out of the idea. "Mom."

"Bring the book, you can work on the bus?" She offered a solution that had sufficed in the past. He sighed. "Stay home and work?" His head shook back and forth slowly. "Leave and let your big brain work on the problem, and it will be sorted out when you get home all sweaty and body-tired?"

His chin jerked up and he stared at her, eyes round in shock. "That's really smart."

"You say that like you're surprised," she scoffed with a grin. "Come on, let's go. We've got—" She pulled her phone out, and thumbed the welcome screen to life. "—three minutes to catch the bus." He came off the bed in a rush and slammed into her, arms around her hips. "Hey, there. I know you." Hands on his shoulders, she walked backwards, leading him out of the room before directing him gently towards the door, shoving the envelope into her back pocket. "You're the kid who's not gonna be late."

They sat on the bus, having made it just before the driver closed the doors, taking their seats still laughing like crazy people at how close it had been. Nate leaned into her side and she lifted an arm, circling his shoulders. "I love you, Nate." The bus jerked and slowed, the sound of the air brakes pulsing through the air.

Nate shifted, getting closer as he looked up. "Will you love the new baby?"

His quiet question was so unexpected she simply stared at him for a moment, unsure. *Do I tell him the truth and have him wonder how I could give away someone I love, or—* She cut off the thought because she tried not to lie to Nate. "Yes, I will love it." He kept his eyes on her, intent on her words. "There are different kinds of love, honey. Even in families with tons of kids, the parents don't love the kids the same. The love I have for you is part of me. The love I have for Uncle Jacob, it's part of me, too. But it's not the same part. Sometimes loving people is about making sure you give them the best you have, and the things they need. I love your Uncle Jacob, but when he needed to go and live with Uncle Trent, I didn't argue."

"Like you could have. Uncle Jakey is a beast when he's on a mission." Nate's brow furrowed. "You wanted him to stay here?"

"Of course, that's the selfish kind of love, though. I wanted him to never leave. But that wouldn't be good for him. And it wouldn't have been good for Uncle Trent." Jaime chewed on her lip for a moment, trying to find the right words. "I would have gotten what I wanted, but it would have cost them."

Nate's eyes widened and he nodded. Something she'd said made sense. *Thank God.* "Necessary and sufficient conditions. I get it. You love Uncle Jake and want him happy. He makes you happy and is happy with you. He would have been happy here, but Uncle Trent makes him happiest. Uncle Jake's happiness matters to you, so the quotient of his happiness was greater if you didn't try and make him stay, even if that meant you didn't have as much happiness. Him being happy made you happier even if he wasn't here."

Jaime chewed her lip again, trying to follow his logic. "Uh, yeah. Him being happiest makes me happy, even if that happiest comes at the cost of me missing him like crazy."

"So you'll love the baby like that." Nate's cheeks pushed up, his smile so wide he was squinting. "That makes sense." He looked down a moment, and when he glanced back up, his lips were pulled to the side, giving her a lopsided grin. "You're smart, Mom."

"And you're a smart-butt." She dug her fingers into his side, glancing up and looking around when he laughed loudly, successfully squirming away. "Next stop is ours, buddy. Big ole church coming up. And then—" She paused, leaning close. "—basketball."

Inside the church, they followed the posted signs leading to the back of the structure and hurried down a corridor, turning a corner to see a gymnasium that stretched the length of the building. There were at least a four dozen kids already in groups, but Jaime was relieved to see a fair number of boys still wandering around. *Not late*, she thought.

A tall man stood to one side, watching the milling groups with a small smile on his face. With a whistle around his neck, he looked the part, so she assumed he must be the organizer of this program, which was new to their neighborhood. Nate trailed behind her a few steps as she made her way towards the man, giving her a moment to take in the masculine beauty in front of her. His sculpted forearms were folded across his chest, bringing her attention to the defined muscles of his entire upper torso. As she got closer, he glanced at her and she was startled by a sense of recognition. *I don't think I know him*, she thought, studying his face for a moment, still feeling like she should. Clean-shaven, his jaw was firm and square, and his brown eyes looked at her, gaze holding steady. "Hi," she began and waved a hand towards Nate, "he's nine. Where does he need to be?"

"Does nine have a name?" The gravel-filled voice stroked through the air and Jaime shivered. "Or can I name him?"

She laughed, and hated the way it sounded, airy and flirty when that was far from how she felt. Tearing her eyes away from him, she stared down at her son. *Remember, this is Nate's coach. He probably has hordes of basketball moms hitting on him. Tone it down, woman.* "Nate. His name is Nate Grimes."

A hand extended past her, and she watched as Nate gripped it in return, pumping solemnly two or three times. "Good to meet you, Nate. I'm Coach."

"Hey, Coach." Nate's smile lit up his face like it always did. "I'm ready to go."

"I can see you are." Coach moved a step closer. Jaime could see his feet and legs, watched with fascination as they shifted towards her. "Eight through ten are in the far corner. We've got some good competition, Nate. You played ball before?'

"Yes, sir." Nate's chest puffed out proudly. "I like basketball best." Jaime grinned, and he looked up at her. "What, Mom?"

"Nothing, honey." *He liked studying best*, she thought, *but basketball comes in a close second*. Without looking at the coach, she turned and waved to where several other parents were perched on a set of fold-out bleachers nearby. "I'll be over here."

She was walking away when she overheard Coach ask Nate, "Mom have a name?" Rolling her eyes, she didn't wait to hear Nate's response. Seated on the narrow bench, she pulled out the envelope she'd retrieved from Nate's jacket before leaving their apartment. When he got home from school, he'd told her Solon had stopped him in the lobby and asked him to bring it up to her.

Opening it, she pulled out a single sheet of paper and stared at it in disbelief. The first words were large and black, centered at the top of the page. Eviction notice.

Connor

Connor scowled down at the clipboard in his hands. He was supposed to be working with the older boys, having arranged this with his assistants before the clinic started. They never knew how many kids would actually show up to these clinics, so, long ago he'd established a protocol that everyone could recite in their sleep. Kids were divided by age, with those divisions getting smaller as the kids got older, and bigger. That helped keep the groups more evenly matched, physically at least. Talent didn't discriminate, and a kid with the juice at eleven or twelve could still run circles around a sixteen-year-old. It'd piss off the teenager, and then he'd court injuries if they retaliated, so Connor kept the older kids together.

Distracted, he had nearly let his group get out of control, and was now working to bring them back without being a dick about it. "Good," he called, pointing at one boy. "Do that again, slower, show the group how to make the crossover work for you." He'd seeded this group with a couple of kids he knew, talking them into coming tonight. He grinned. Not that it took a lot of persuasion to convince someone who loved the game to take advantage of some free coaching time.

Glancing across the gym, he watched his friend working with the eight to ten boys. A grade school PE teacher, originally Miles had been scheduled for the group just under the ones Connor was working with. When the kid, Nate, had shown aptitude, Connor had shifted things on the fly, glad he didn't have to make up a story to get Miles on the kid.

Connor motioned to one of the roving assistants, telling him, "Keep them focused on passing. Do another set of one-hand passing, then a set of catch, dribble, pass." Stepping to put his back against the wall, he turned his full attention to the other end of the gym. To anyone watching him, it would look like he was observing the entire practice. In reality, he only had eyes for the blonde in the bleachers. Jaime Grimes. Marie and Cooper's surrogate.

Her reaction when she came in didn't tell him anything about her. Nothing except that she had not the faintest clue who he was. He hadn't wanted to tip her off and was glad he'd introduced himself simply as Coach. Nate would have called him that anyway, or at the most Coach T, like a lot of the kids did. Jaime, however, didn't call him anything. After she'd eye fucked him, she'd studiously ignored him. He had ceased to exist for her, and that bugged him in a different way.

He'd been staring at her for several minutes before he realized she wasn't moving. She wasn't seeing anything. Not really. Face fixed forwards, someone could have been fooled that she was watching Nate's group. When the other kids executed a move, their parents would straighten and glance around, hoping someone else had seen their offspring excel against their peers. Not Jaime. For as involved as she'd been when she and her kid had entered the gym together, right now she was lost inside her own head.

Connor narrowed his eyes, seeing a piece of paper in her hand. Her other hand was curled into a loose fist, tucked under her chin, elbow propped on her knee. Bent over as she was, it looked almost like she was feeling ill.

He strolled the length of the gym, talking to the assistants as he went, but his focus remained on Jaime. She didn't move the entire time he was walking. It had been a week since she was at Cooper's. Maybe they'd started the process and the paper was bad news. What if she wasn't a good candidate after everything Cooper and Marie had been through? Connor grimaced. If it was bad news, he wanted to know before Cooper did, so he could try and soften the blow. He drifted in her direction, coming to a stop next to the bleachers. Surreptitiously, he eyed the paper, pulling in a hard breath when he saw why she was frozen. Evicted from her apartment.

Fuck.

He glanced over at Nate, seeing the boy had noticed his mother's distress finally and was on his way toward them. Reaching up, Connor snatched the paper from her fingers and crumpled it, shoving it into the pocket of his jacket. Nate took two bounding steps up the bleachers, his tone worried beyond anything Connor would have expected, asked, "Mom, are you okay?"

Connor had shocked her with his action and he could see the fear on her features, then she carefully smoothed her expression and faced Nate. "Right as rain, honey. You're doing great." She smiled, but something must have been off because Nate wasn't buying what she was trying to sell.

"Something's wrong." Chin out, Nate demanded, "What's wrong, Mom?"

"Nothing I can't fix." Connor shifted so he could see her face, where the determination on her features backed up her confident statement. "Now go, don't waste Coach's time." Nate hesitated, and she smiled, this one more genuine as she reassured the boy, "Nothing I can't fix. I promise."

She waited for Nate to get all the way back across the gym and to his group before she turned to Connor. "May I have that back, please?" She'd projected confidence for Nate, but was more fragile than she wanted to admit, and her voice wavered for an instant, turning her request into a plea. Connor studied her, watched how she pressed her lips together and knew it was to keep them from quivering.

Slowly he shook his head.

She closed her eyes and dropped her chin to her chest, fighting for control in a public place.

He was an ass for making her go through this, but he had a feeling. One he hadn't experienced in a long time. She pulled in a shuddering breath, and he watched as a single tear broke free, trailing down her cheek, that shimmering droplet reflecting the gym's lights. His skin tingled as it traveled to her jaw, hanging there for a moment before it dropped to her shirt. "Please. If you saw what it said, you know what I'm dealing with. Please." Her lips parted as she took another broken breath. "Don't do this. I don't even know you. Please."

"Let me help." He didn't know what he was going to say when he opened his mouth, but once the words were out, they felt right. "Let me help you."

Expression twisting, she looked anguished as she squeezed her eyes tightly for a moment then opened them and lifted her chin, staring into his face. "No, thank you." One small hand extended, she repeated her request. "May I have that back, please?"

Damn. Crystal blue eyes framed with tear-clumped lashes, she held his gaze. *She doesn't look anything like Marie*, he thought. Marie was pretty, but this woman was beautiful. And this woman, this gorgeous,

65

compassionate, fierce, protective woman and mother, did not want his help.

Digging in his pocket, he pulled out the wadded ball of paper and handed it back.

Bet she'll accept it from Coop and Marie.

Chapter Seven

Jaime

"What do you mean there's an advance payment?" Jaime stared at Sarah, no less confused than she'd been this morning when she checked her bank balance to find it was thousands of dollars healthier than it had been in years. She had spent hours racking her brain, trying to figure this out. The deposit was clearly from the clinic, but it didn't make any sense. It still didn't. "Everything is in escrow until we have the sonogram with the heartbeat." That was what the paperwork all said. She was certain of it. She'd read it three times this morning alone. "We're not scheduled for the first procedure until tomorrow."

Sarah smiled at her. "In most cases, yes. Because the Thompsons have been through the process before, there's an exception."

"An exception?" Jaime shook her head. The money was a windfall, because it would allow her to move to a better apartment immediately, screw the eviction notice and screw Solon. She already had a line on a different place. But she couldn't spend it if there was a chance it would be rescinded. "What does that mean?"

"Maybe bonus is a better word." Sarah tapped for several moments on her keyboard, and the printer behind her whirred to life. "I should have had you sign this before I authorized the transfer, but I knew you'd be coming in tomorrow." She shrugged and whirled to grab the single sheet of paper off the tray. Sliding it across the desk, she flashed a broad smile that held just a tiny bit of unease which did nothing to settle Jaime's nerves. "I didn't expect to see you today, but here, you can sign it now." Sarah took a pen from the holder near her computer, laying it beside the paper.

"Tell me why there's a bonus I didn't know about." Jaime didn't look down, didn't break eye contact. This meant she saw the tiny bit of unease grow into a flare. "It's not illegal, is it?" The relief Sarah showed her was real. So it wasn't illegal, but it was out of the norm, which made Jaime nervous.

"No, not illegal," Sarah confirmed. "Not at all. It is…unexpected. But then again you and the Thompsons have made a strong connection in the weeks you've known each other. It's only natural they want to thank you for what you're doing in the only way they really can." One corner of her mouth quirked up as she said, "Personally, I think it's beyond sweet. That paper"—she pointed to the sheet still lying on the desk—"is an addendum to the contract. It doesn't call it a bonus. The legal language doesn't allow for that. It's a compensation increase with an advance. Covers everyone that way." Tipping her head to one side, she paused a moment and her face softened as she quietly said, "It's a good thing, Jaime."

After spending two sleepless nights fruitlessly trying to figure out how to stay in their apartment, Jaime did the only thing she could. She burst into tears, burying her face in her hands.

Connor

"Need any reading material?" Cooper's voice was amused as he tapped Connor's shoulder with his fist. Amused, but tight, exposing the emotion that had him in its grip. They were at the clinic, waiting.

"No, man. I got this." Connor held up his phone, waggling it back and forth. "I'm the jizz master, brother. All the material I could need, right here in this tiny, mysterious box they call a smartphone." He snorted a laugh. "Jesus, Coop."

Frowning, Cooper said, "You're quick on the draw with that." A look of concern flashed across his face. "You abstained, right?"

Rolling his eyes, knowing it was nerves that were driving his brother crazy, Connor laughed. "Yeah, bro. I told you, I got this. Not my first rodeo. I've gone without my hand for a week now. We're good, Coop. Swear."

"I know. I hate the waiting. Sorry." Cooper shook his head and leaned back in the uncomfortable chair. "I can't thank you enough, Connor. This means—"

Connor cut him off with a gesture. "We've had this convo. Anything for you, bro."

A knock sounded on the door and he chuckled, knowing it would be Marie. He gripped Cooper's bicep and squeezed before he called out, "Oh, baby, do it again. That feels so good."

"Connor Allen Thompson, you don't scare me. I'll come in anyway." Marie scolded through the door as he reached over to flip the lock on the doorknob. She pushed into the room. Sized for one, with three occupants it was now claustrophobic. Eyes only for Cooper, Marie breathed, "She's here."

Cooper asked, "She prepped yet?" The egg retrieval procedure was today, which was why Connor's presence was required. He didn't have to be here, could have done his collection days ago and dropped it off to be frozen. That's how they'd done things with Sam, but since then he'd read articles that suggested this was the better route.

His part was easy.

Connor glanced at the collection cup he'd placed on the table in the corner. Little tug, little pull, little imagination—he'd have the cup half-filled in no time. He thought about Jaime, calling up an image of her face. Not when she'd been crying and frustrated at him being an apparent bullying asshole, but when she first had gotten to the gym with Nate, and her innocent flirting had captured his attention along with his sudden knowledge of who she was. He felt his cock start to fatten and bit back a curse.

She'd occupied his thoughts these past few days. After practice had ended, he had followed her and Nate outside, watched them wait for and then climb on the bus, their comfortable chatter telling him this was a standard mode of transportation. Nate had been animated, hands and body flung here and there as he described what he'd done that night. Once Connor had locked up after all the kids and parents were gone home, he'd gone straight to Cooper's house and told him what he'd found out, then followed it with his idea.

"Come on, Coop. She wouldn't take it from me. But you didn't see her with that boy, man. This is a woman who just needs a fucking break. I got the money, you know I do. Marie would totally be down with the idea." Connor knew he was scowling, but he hadn't expected to get any resistance. *"Want me to talk to her instead? She's gotten to be friends with Jaime, she'll agree with me in a heartbeat."*

"Fuck you," Cooper shot back.

"She just needs a break. You didn't see the worry on her face. The smallest of breaks, man. I can give her one." He didn't want to talk about the motive behind this, content to let Cooper believe it was about the baby.

Instead it was much more. It was about having that hole in his heart gone for the few short minutes he'd been talking to her, a sense of completeness he hadn't known existed until Cole died and he lost it.

"We'll have to tell Marie." That was the signal for Cooper's surrender, and Connor grinned, knowing he'd won.

His part would consist of thinking of her, mostly.

Her part, much harder.

IVs and meds, nurses and techs hovering around her, she'd be scarcely covered by the thin gown as she lay on her back. Lot of trust there, wide open for anyone to see, sedated. He'd read articles about this, too; there was danger involved for an egg donor, and he wondered suddenly why they were doing it in vitro and not intrauterine. *Jesus, my brain.*

"They're doing the final interview." Marie's words pulled him out of his thoughts and he blinked at her. "Prep next. I just wanted to give you an update. Since she's in the building, you could—" Marie paused a beat and grinned at Connor. "—you know. Get started."

"Jesus, woman. Did you just tell my baby brother to jack off?" Cooper stood and herded her towards the door, Connor's laughter following both of them. "That ain't right." The closing door cut off anything else Cooper might have been going to say.

Hand to the knob, Connor locked the door and leaned back, eyeing the container. *Showtime.*

Jaime

"No, I don't have anyone." In tears, Jaime looked at the nurse. "I don't drive, though. I take the bus. That's okay, right?" Since the treatments had started, her emotions had been all over the place, and she'd found herself crying at the drop of a hat. Thirty-six hours ago on the nose, she'd been in this same room, bent over, ass in the air, waiting on the shot that would trigger her eggs. "Why didn't anyone say anything?"

"I'm sorry, Mrs. Grimes."

Jaime shook her head and corrected her, suddenly angry instead of devastated. "It's Miss, not Mrs."

The nurse picked up smoothly, telling Jaime by her actions and easy manner that she didn't think Jaime was nutso. This behavior was obviously normal in fertilityland. "Miss Grimes, I don't know why it wasn't explained specifically, but I do know it's in the paperwork we provide. We ask that you bring an adult who can accompany you home and stay with you for just the first couple of hours."

"Well, I don't have anyone." Admitting that was harder than she expected, which was likely why she'd apparently glossed over the information in the packet. "I thought that was just to drive, and like I said, I don't drive."

"Let me just step out and tell the Thompsons." At the nurse's words, Jaime's throat clogged with renewed

73

tears. Three weeks of treatments thrown away because she didn't have a friend to call.

Connor

"Bro." A knock came from the door just as Connor screwed the lid on the container. "Don't bother." Anger and frustration flooded through him at the defeated tone in his brother's voice. "We're not a go."

"I thought the ultrasound showed she had several eggs ready?" Connor used a wipe he'd already taken out of the package to clean his cock, then tucked himself away, straightening his boxers before fastening his pants. *Another month of these motherfuckers*, he thought in annoyance as he wiped his fingers and tossed the trash.

"She does. There's a wrinkle." Connor unlocked the door and yanked it open, suddenly certain he knew what the wrinkle was. *Shit. Totally fucking read her wrong. Didn't think she was that type.*

"Oh, I bet there's a wrinkle." He stared at Cooper, seeing the lines of fatigue in his features.

"No, it's not her backing out. If anything, she's more upset than anyone else, even Marie." Cooper sighed. "She doesn't have anyone to stay with her. We, Marie and I, could take her to a hotel, but she started freaking out about her son. She's just upset and not thinking straight. I guess there's something tonight that he doesn't want to miss, and she promised him they'd go. She thought the whole 'bring an adult with you' was just to drive, and since she takes the bus everywhere—" He shrugged and sighed. "—she didn't think it applied. We'll sort it out for next month."

"She needs a ride?" Connor clipped out the words in disbelief. "We're scrapping this month because she needs a fucking ride and a babysitter?"

"She's upset, Connor. Marie's in with her now, but she's not backing out."

"I'll do it." Connor lifted his chin as Cooper stared at him. "She needs a ride, I'm it. Needs a babysitter, I'm there, too. Nate needs a ride to practice, I'm his ride. No problem." He swallowed, not sure how he felt about the idea of spending so many hours with Jaime when he'd just used her image to jack off to. "I'm there, bro. Maybe I should...officially meet her."

Excitement lighting his face, without answering, Cooper angled a finger to point at the specimen cup. Connor leaned into the room and grabbed it, then turned to follow him up the hallway. He stopped at the window to pass it off to the tech, then walked to where Cooper had stopped in front of a door. He could hear sobs of "I'm so sorry," through the thin wood and as he listened found himself absently scrubbing at his sternum.

Cooper glanced at him and said, "Wait here," then lifted one hand and rapped on the door. Connor heard soft voices, and Jaime's hiccupping sobs slowly died off, becoming softer and less frequent. After a moment, Marie called, "Come in."

The door closed behind Cooper, and Connor was left standing alone in the hallway, but only for a moment before Marie was in front of him, tear-streaked face studying him. "She's upset." Connor nodded. "Be nice." When he didn't respond, her brows inched together, and the tiny wrinkle appeared between them that Cooper called her "I want" line.

Connor smiled and cupped her face in his hands, bringing her close so he could kiss it away. "Love you, little sister. I'll be nice."

She moved and he stepped through the door to see Jaime seated next to the tiny desk, a handful of tissues held to her face. "Jaime," he said, "I'm Coach Thompson." When he spoke her name, she shivered and lowered the tissues, her eyes widening in incredulity when they landed on him.

"Oh. My. God." Her pauses were distinct, and he tried not to grin at how cute that was. "You're Coach. The coach from basketball. Nate's coach." He lost his battle with the grin, and when she frowned in response, he smiled wider. "Cooper said you would drive me home."

Cooper must have left off the babysitting and shuttling to and from practice, but he wouldn't rock the boat at this point. "Yes. If that's the only thing standing in the way of this thing moving forwards, I'm happy to be your personal cabbie today." He took a step closer and squatted, putting one knee to the floor, bringing his face level with hers. "From talking to Coop and Marie, I know that you're all-in on this, and I want you to know I am, too. The three of us"—without looking back, he gestured

behind him, indicating his brother and sister-in-law—
"have been in this together. Jaime, now you're in it with
us, too. This is the least I can do." He took a breath and
held it, waiting.

She nodded, and Marie gave a strangled cry. Jaime's
eyes never left Connor's face. "Okay. They said that I
need someone for a couple of hours." Her hard swallow
was audible. This was a woman not accustomed to asking
for anything. "Could you...?"

"As long as is needed. Tonight is practice so I can
drive all of us there, too."

"Okay." This time it came faster and he smiled.

Cooper muttered, "I'll go talk to the office." The
door opened and closed.

"Thank you." Even without looking, he knew Marie
had gone with Cooper. "What you're doing for them.
It's...it means an awful lot to a bunch of people."

"They are genuinely good people." Her eyes grew
bright and she fluttered a hand in front of her face.
"Sorry. I do this all the time now." She sniffed, and he
tugged a couple of tissues from a box on the desk,
passing them over. "As you witnessed the other night.
Sorry about that." She waved the tissues. "I'm not
normally like this."

"You seem to be genuinely good people, too." At his
words, her eyes got bright again and she looked to the
side. *Okay, douche, don't make the ovulating chick cry.*

77

All women liked talking about their kids, right? "Nate's a good kid. I was impressed by him last week."

"The best." She gave a tiny laugh, but her smile was big. *Score with the topic change*. "He's a character. Love him."

"Have you met Sam yet? He's the best little guy. Gutsy and fierce, he's gonna give Coop a run for his money when he's older." He liked how her face softened at that. "Nate told me he's in high school?" That had been a surprise, and he had wondered if Nate was lying when Connor asked him why he didn't know any of the kids his own age. "He's nine, right?"

She nodded, lips quivering again and he wondered why talking about her son would bring on the tears afresh. "He takes after his daddy in the brains department. Brice was a musical prodigy, could have done anything, but the mathematics of music composition spoke to his soul." She'd said "was" and now he understood how it was she had such empathy for his family's loss. "Brice was killed in a car wreck when I was pregnant with Nathan. He never got to see his son. He would be so proud of Nate."

"Nine years old and in high school. Man, that's amazing. What's he interested in, other than basketball?" He shook his head. "This explains a lot, because I was stumped how he was deconstructing the drills. He spent a few minutes trying to tell one of the assistant coaches how to change things to get more benefit." Connor laughed. "When it got back to me, I validated the theory, not knowing until afterwards it came from a nine-year-old. I planned on talking to him tonight, explain why college-level drills weren't appropriate for grade school players."

"He's opinionated and doesn't have the maturity to filter through what he reads. Sometimes he gets ahead of himself." She was smiling now, at least, and he liked the look on her far better than the tears. "He's very into science right now. All of this"—she waved her hand at her belly—"probably doesn't help."

"He knows what's going on?" Connor snorted a laugh. "Never mind. Don't answer that. Of course he does. Some kids you could hide a pregnancy from, but not if he's that smart. You have your job cut out for you, little lady."

The door swung open followed by a belated knock, and Connor turned around to see a nurse standing there. Her eyes went back and forth between them as she smiled warmly. "I'm glad to see you were able to call a friend in, Miss Grimes. We're ready for you." Turning to Connor, she said, "Partners can come back and be with the patient until we're ready to begin, then you'll have to go to the waiting room. Sorry."

"Oh, he's—"

Connor spoke over Jaime, cutting her off. "Sounds good." From his position on the floor, he had to look up slightly. There was an expression of uncertainty on her face as he echoed his earlier thoughts. "You're doing the hard part. Least I can do is hold your hand."

Sitting in the waiting room with Cooper and Marie was the longest hour of his life until the doctor came out. "Five eggs. We've already introduced the sperm to the container. Now we see what they look like in a few days."

Connor waited a minute, but while the doctor kept talking, it was just going through the process again with Marie and Cooper. Everything he said was about the procedure, and nothing else. "How's Jaime?"

"The donor? She did well. She'll be in recovery for a while, then be released to go home." He turned to Marie, holding out his hand to say goodbye.

Hearing her coldly referred to like that was something Connor found he didn't like it at all. "Jaime," he said insistently, and the doctor turned to look at him. "Her name is Jaime. Can I go see her?"

"Oh, I'm sorry. I thought you were with the Thompsons. Yes, of course, I'll take you back."

Slightly mollified, Connor followed the doctor to the area set aside for recovery without glancing at Cooper and Marie. Jaime was in a hospital bed, rails raised, head turned to the side. Lips parted slightly, she was snoring lightly, hair still half-tucked in the cap they'd put on her before he'd been forced to leave her earlier. *Beautiful, loyal, smart, loving. She's funny, too.* Standing next to the bed, he stared down at her, watching her sleep while he tried to sort out what was in his head.

Jaime

Still drowsy due to the sleepless nights caused by a combination of her financial situation and dreading the procedure, Jaime was dozing on the couch when she heard the front door. "Hey, bud," she called softly, not wanting Nate to worry about seeing her on the couch when she'd normally be bustling around the kitchen.

Connor had left a few minutes ago to run an errand, promising to return and pick up Nate for practice. She squinted, trying to see the clock on the front of the microwave, finding to her surprise Connor had been gone more than an hour. She lay her head back down with a sigh of relief, feeling the wings of sleep folding back around her. Thankfully, the nausea that had plagued her all day wasn't as bad when she was entirely prone.

Noise somewhere in the apartment woke her again and she assumed it was Nate, so she called a question, "Homework?"

"All done." She rolled to her side to find Nate's face right in front of her. He was seated on the floor beside the couch, already dressed in his basketball clothes.

"Didn't you just get home?" Shifting, she held out a hand and he grabbed it tightly. "I'm sorry I was sleeping, buddy. Did you get a snack?"

"Mom, I just got home from practice." Belatedly she realized his hair was wet, streaks of perspiration on the shirt, too.

There was a soft buzz of voices in the apartment and she twisted, trying to see over the arm of the couch. "Hello?"

"Just me," Connor said, striding into view and crouching beside where Nate sat. "How you feeling, Jaime?"

"Confused." She cleared her throat. "Was someone here?"

"Marie. She stayed with you while Nate and I went to practice." He moved, holding out a hand, putting his palm on her forehead. "Are you hungry yet?"

"I am," Nate piped up. "Starved."

She got to watch as this beautiful man turned his full attention on her son and smiled at him with affection. The only other man who had ever looked at Nate like that was her brother. Affection and tolerance, combined with a warmth that seemed soul deep. Connor's smile turned to a mischievous grin as he said, "Good thing we got two double supreme pizzas, then."

"Marie was here?" Connor turned back to her and nodded. She realized his hand was still on her forehead, his fingers absently brushing through her hair. "I'm sorry. I'm still confused."

"Nate, the pizzas are on top of the oven. Wanna make your mom and me a plate, then make one for yourself?" From the corner of her eye, she saw her son nod and then get up, disappearing behind Connor as he went to the kitchen. "You've been sick off and on since we got home. There was no way you could make basketball. I figured if Nate had to miss the clinic tonight, you'd feel even worse once you realized." He smiled at her. "I could have called one of my assistants to pick him up and run practice for me while I stayed here, but I didn't have your permission. I know Marie, and she would have kicked my ass if I'd left you here alone and something had happened. She said you slept the whole time I was gone."

Jaime struggled to get an elbow underneath her, trying to push up to a sitting position. Connor moved close and wrapped an arm around her back. He held her when she swayed, the room spinning around her. She swallowed, fighting nausea. "I'm sorry." *He was just supposed to bring me home.* She swallowed again.

"Coach, you want to eat at the table?" Nate called from the kitchen.

"Yeah, bud, just gimme a minute." Connor's voice turned quiet, pitched for her ears only when he asked, "You gonna get sick, Jaime? We can go to the bathroom if you need." She shook her head, then nodded as bitter fluid flooded her mouth. He was up in a single movement, arm under her legs, cradling her to his chest as he carried her to the bathroom. "Hold on, Jaim."

He placed her on the edge of the tub and leaned over, lifting the toilet cover and ring. One hand on her arm, holding her in place while she retched, he stretched and grabbed a clean cloth from the stack in an open cabinet. He dropped it in the sink and flipped the faucet to cold, letting the water run over the cloth. She sat up and reached to wipe her mouth with the back of her hand and he beat her to it, the cold rag feeling good against her skin.

"They said this was normal. When I called, I mean." Seated on the edge of the tub beside her, he was so much taller she had to look up into his face. "If we can get some food into you, they said it will probably get better. Nate and I stopped at the store on the way home, and I picked up the soups he said you liked."

"You called the clinic?" He nodded. "And bought food?" He nodded again. "I'm so sorry. I know you didn't expect this to turn into an extended stay like this. I'll pay you back." She took the cloth from him, suddenly aware that he was still using it to stroke her forehead and cheeks. Pushing to her feet, she leaned against the counter to turn on the cold water and scooped a handful into her mouth to rinse out the sour taste. Spitting discreetly, she swirled water around the sink, then continued, "For everything."

"Pizza and soup won't break me, Jaim." That was the second time she'd heard him call her that, and she liked it. It was almost like Jacob's nickname for her, James. She'd noticed he'd picked up her nickname for Nate, too, calling him "bud" earlier. *He probably nicknames everyone*, she thought. *Isn't that something coaches do?* "Let's get something in your belly before you blow away."

That was it, she realized. She knew she was thin, and he probably thought that could present problems for the pregnancy. Before she could react, he had scooped her up again, carrying her to the couch. "I can get my soup. You should eat the pizza before it gets cold. I'm feeling much better now, wide awake. I'm sure pizza isn't your favorite pick for dinner. If you'd like to leave, Nate and I will be fine." She pushed at his chest, surprised when his arms tightened around her instead of releasing. "Please."

He ignored that as well and instead, settled her on the couch before tucking the blanket in around her legs. Bending so he was close, he asked her, "Pizza or soup?"

"Connor—"

He shook his head, an expression she didn't understand on his face as he repeated, "Pizza or soup?"

Jaime pressed her lips together and watched as his gaze dropped to her mouth, his eyes darkening before he looked back into her eyes. "Soup." He'd moved closer, and there were only a few inches between them when she blurted, "What kind of soup did you get?"

"Chicken tortellini and a turkey bean. Got a preference between the two? Nate assured me they were your favorites." He moved, and she thought he was going to touch her again; then his hand fell away as he straightened, unfolding to his full height.

"Chicken tortellini. Nate didn't steer you wrong."

He smiled then, the corner of his mouth quirking up in a quick grin. "Good to know. One bowl of soup, coming up." Lifting his head, he called out as he moved to the kitchen, "Nate, bud, did you save me any pizza?"

She wasn't lying, she did feel better. And then after she ate the soup Nate brought her, carefully balancing the full bowl between hands covered by oven mitts, she felt even better.

Connor

Jesus, man. What in the actual fuck am I thinking? After staying until Nate's bedtime, he'd left Jaime with a promise of help if she needed him. Twenty minutes later, he was still sitting in the cab of his truck in the parking lot, staring up at the building Jaime and Nate lived in. The entire structure was flat, no windows to break the monotony of the red and white brick and mortar. No light, no air, and until now, no hope.

Talking to Nate was a revelation, because he found Jaime was entirely correct about her son. He was brilliant beyond anything Connor had ever known, so smart it took some getting used to. He was a genius, but he was also nine years old. That meant he didn't know what was, and was not okay to talk about when it came to his mother.

Out of work. Selling plasma to buy groceries. Taking cash jobs to pay rent. Doing all of that and still being there for her kid when he needed her. Making sure Nate had every chance he deserved, putting her boy first in everything.

It wouldn't surprise Connor to find out she'd started down the path to surrogate because of the money. *Uterus for rent.* His mouth twisted in anger at the idea she'd been driven to that by desperation. Even as he thought that, he knew it wasn't like that for her now. Not after meeting Cooper and Marie. She was a woman on a mission.

Nate's dad came from money. She shouldn't have had to struggle like this to raise his son. Nate's grandparents on that side of the family sounded like total assholes. Connor leaned forwards, resting his forehead against his crossed wrists on the steering wheel.

Jaime's family was better, but not here. She sounded so stubborn Connor was certain they didn't have a clue how things were for her. Her brother would be here in a heartbeat, based on what Nate said about his uncle.

Single mom, making things work all on her own. Just like a thousand others like her.

They weren't like her, though. *Never met anybody like her.* He snorted. *How can I feel like I've known her my whole life, when I really just met her today?*

He straightened and shoved the key into the slot, twisting until the engine roared. *She's not on her own anymore.*

Chapter Eight
Connor

Seated at his desk, he stared down at the phone resting between his hands. On the screen was Jaime's number, entered into his phone by Nate last night at Connor's request. An excuse of, "So I can let her know about practice," enough for the kid. He'd forced himself to wait all day, eyes to the clock in each classroom like a horny boy on a Friday afternoon. Impatient for the day to be over with so he could talk to the object of his fascination. In that boy's world, there would be a girl with flirty moves, hair flips and batting eyes, girlfriends who clustered around and giggled at everything the fledgling couple said or did. For Connor, it was the chance to hear her voice again, to listen to her talk about anything at all.

Remember, asswipe, she's Coop's surrogate.

Right, like his cock had remembered that this morning when he'd had to tug one out in the shower, hard as a rock at the memory of watching her sleep on her lousy, lumpy couch.

I'm just checking on her.

Right, because the clinic wouldn't have done that. The memory of her throwing up rocketed to the top of his thoughts, not a sexy memory, but she'd been so sick it had scared him. It had scared Nate, too, and that bugged Connor, not liking how the boy had paled when he'd got home from school to find his mother on the couch with a bowl nearby.

With a growl, he grabbed the phone and locked it, tossing it back to the desktop. He opened his roster on the computer, working through his first string for an upcoming game. When he realized he'd put the same kid down twice, he growled again and snagged the phone.

Not giving himself time to think, he went to her number and pushed the Call button.

"Hello?" Her voice was strong and sweet, the uplifted tone questioning who would be calling her was so cute he forgot to answer for a moment. "Hello? Is anyone there?"

"Jaime," he sounded choked, and cleared his throat. "Hi, it's Connor."

"Connor." She sounded worried, and he wondered why. Then she said, "Is everything okay? Are Marie and Cooper okay?"

"Coop? Yeah. He's… they're fine, I'm sure. I haven't heard anything…I just called to check on you. See how you're doing." He paused, then rolled his eyes at his own lameness. "So how are you? Doing, I mean?"

Sounding slightly confused, Jaime said, "I'm well, thank you." She must have thought him calling was a demand for more thanks, because she followed that with, "It was very kind, what you did last night. What with taking me home, and then taking Nate to practice. I'm glad you called, Connor. I'd hoped to have a chance to tell you thank you again." A pause, then he could hear the smile in her voice when she said, "So, thank you."

"Did you have any trouble falling asleep after I left?" He had. He'd gotten home and then climbed into bed, tossing and turning because his brain wouldn't shut off. What if she'd gotten ill again? What if Nate didn't hear her?

Her soft laugh made him catch his breath. "No, I slept like a baby. If it hadn't been for Nate, I would have overslept this morning, in fact."

"Well, I'm glad that didn't happen. It's good that the sickness has passed, yeah?" *Oh good, remind her she was puking in front of me.* "Soup did the trick." *And now she's going to think I'm talking about buying groceries, again.* "I enjoyed playing games with you and Nate. He's a great kid."

There was no discernable tension in her voice when she agreed with him, and he let out a silent whoosh of relieved air. "Yeah, he is pretty awesome." Then she

90

reminded him why this call was a bad idea. "When I told him about being a surrogate and asked him what he wanted me to tell the parents, his first thought was to not tell them about how smart he was. He wanted to focus on basketball, and how he did things without being asked. It's always validating to hear what kids think are the most important things."

"Yeah," he said softly. There was noise in the gym and he looked up to see a row of kids at the window, hands cupped around their faces as they stared in at him. Looking at the clock, he realized he was ten minutes late starting practice. "Team practice is about to start. I just wanted to check on you, Jaime. Maybe we can do another night in like that sometime soon."

"I'd like that." Her voice was a near whisper. "Goodbye."

"Bye."

Jaime

Three days, three calls from Connor. These conversations had become a regular part of her evening so easily, it was frightening.

"Bye." She ended the call and closed her eyes, resting the phone on her chest for a minute.

When she saw his name on the display, her heart would speed up. Answering the call was worse, because the sound of his voice made her want to close her eyes, focusing on him. It meant in the silences, she could hear the pounding of her own heartbeat.

Tonight had been a difficult conversation. The anniversary of Brice's death was approaching, and she'd made a comment about how calendars didn't have a pause button.

"Don't I know it," Connor said, his voice suddenly gruff. "Holidays and birthdays, everything seems to come at me faster every year."

"It's weird, isn't it? How when it comes time for a tough anniversary, something you dread, you still want someone to say something? But people don't know what to do, so they don't do anything." She sighed, curling a strand of hair around her finger. "It's like they don't know what's right. Do they mention it and risk reminding you in case you'd forgotten, or do they ignore it, and give you space to ignore it, too?"

"Yeah. When all you want is to be able to tell someone, 'Hey, I'm glad you remember, too.'" He was quiet for a minute, then asked, "What was Nate's dad like?"

"Brice? Best guy in the world." Jaime felt her lips curl into a smile. "We were high school sweethearts. So sappy. When I look back, it's crazy how in love we were."

"His parents didn't approve, did they?" He didn't hold any censure in his tone; this was just an inquiry for him. Nothing more. She told herself he didn't know what she'd been like. Jaime had been Brice's girlfriend, not a care in the world. All of that was so far from her life now it could have happened on a different planet.

"No, they didn't like me. Not for their boy." She shifted, turning to her side, propping the phone underneath her head. "He was destined for greatness. I heard his daddy say those words a thousand times. 'Destined for greatness,' when all Brice wanted was the music. It mattered to him, because it was beautiful."

"And you mattered to him, too." Connor's tone was rich, low and vibrating, and she didn't know what to do with the implied compliment, that she was important because she was beautiful.

"He loved me. Told me he knew the moment we met." Sadness suffused her at these bittersweet memories. "Worst day of my life, hearing the news that he was dead." She swallowed, her mouth suddenly dry. "Losing someone is hard. You know how it is. One day they're there, talking and laughing and planning."

"And the next moment they are gone." Connor's voice had gone flat and hollow, his words clipped. "I knew when Cole died. Knew the minute he died. We were twins, did you know?"

"Yeah," she whispered, because anything louder would have been disrespectful.

"I think it was my fault." Not a whisper, but his words sounded strangled, and she suddenly wished they weren't on the phone, but that she was standing in front of him, and could hold him, and comfort him. "We'd always done everything together. He'd never had to worry about watching his back, because I was there. Unspoken, we'd have the other, come hell or high water."

"You can't believe that, Con." Jaime shook her head, denying his words with every fiber of her being. "You can't know if you'd been there what the outcome would have been."

"I can't know it wouldn't have saved him." He was silent for a moment, then repeated his words, "I can't know that, Jaime."

"Nothing can answer that question. Like I can't know if I'd been in the car with Brice, would he have died still? If I'd been there, would we have even been on the road right then? Was me not being there what cost Nate his daddy?" Close to tears, Jaime knew it showed in her voice, the sound of grief something she'd had in her head for so long. "But I can't know that I wouldn't have died, too. We can't go down that path, Con. It's not healthy."

"I don't want to think of you dying, Jaime." Gruff and rough, he sounded near tears, too. "Nate and you are too vital to think of being gone."

"And so are you. You can't let it eat you up. But when anniversaries roll around, like Brice's death, it's hard not to second-guess everything. I think it's these times when having someone to talk to can make a difference." She swallowed hard, holding herself together by a hair, then said, "Thank you for being that person for me today, Connor. Thank you."

Chapter Nine
Connor

"No, Dad, it's not that." Connor shook his head as he tried to fit the oversized wrench to the bolt holding the tranny cover on the back of the tractor. He'd come out to the family farm in Sugarglide, Arkansas, about two hours north and west of Memphis. Since neither he nor Cooper wanted to work the land, in recent years they'd talked their parents into leasing off most of it, but the old man kept about a hundred acres in rice around the old home place. That was where they were today, in a big barn behind the home where the boys had grown up.

"Well, then you should tell me what it is like, because so far all you can say is it's not like this or that or the other." A second wrench tapped Connor's shoulder. "Middle bolt is metric. No idea why they'd do it that way. Doesn't make sense."

"No. It doesn't make sense. I didn't even want to meet her. You heard me talk about it. I thought Coop was crazy, wanting to get to know the gestational carrier the first time. But at least they did an anonymous egg." Connor took the wrench, quickly backing the bolt out of the hole and setting it in the metal bowl beside him. "But if you heard her. She's just...I don't know, Pa. I catch myself thinking about her, wondering what she'd think about whatever it is I'm doing. By the time school's out, I can't get to a phone fast enough. She's not the kind of woman I'd go for. Coop and Cole, yeah. Not me. She's petite... No, scratch that." He reached into the opening and found the sensor wire that had broken, following it by feel back to where it attached to the transmission. "She's small. Not tall, and way too fuc—flogging thin." By habit, he still self-edited his language around his parents. "But her heart is way bigger than you could ever imagine. And how she is with her boy? She's the kind of woman any man would want to mother his kids."

"You're thinking kids already? You even had her on a date?" His dad laughed. "And I meant it didn't make any sense why they'd use both metric and standard on this made-in-America tractor." A wire with a connector dangled in front of Connor's face. "Here's the sensor."

Focused on what his hands were doing, Connor dropped the thread of the conversation. As they were reassembling the cover, his dad picked it back up.

"When I met your mother, you want to know the first thought that flew through my head?" Connor turned to look at his dad as they gathered the tools from the blanket he'd laid on the ground. Without waiting for an answer, his dad said, "That she'd be a good momma. I'd gone to the fair in Memphis, was walking through the livestock barn and there was a little girl who'd fallen, scraped her knee. City people walked on past, but your mom came up and crouched down, wiped at it with the hem of her shirt, bent close to blow air across it. Told the little girl, 'Don't cry, sweetheart.' I thought she knew the girl, but the parents came by right after that, and they thanked Judy. Thanked her for taking care of a stranger.

"I walked up and introduced myself, took her hand. I told her it was sweet what she'd done. She blushed, tried to tell me it was something anyone would do. I knew different because there were at least a dozen folks who walked past. I tucked her hand into the bend of my elbow and strolled the rest of the livestock barns with her. Then I took her to dinner. Wouldn't take any answer other than yes from her. Had to get to know her, and when I did, I knew I was right. From the minute my eyes landed on that woman, I knew. The first time she said my name, and us surrounded by the smell of cows and chickens, I knew. The setting didn't matter, the woman did." He leaned close, gripping Connor's arm. "Listen to your heart, son. You'll know if she's something you want to explore. Ignore the situation. Don't let circumstance rob you of joy. We are not guaranteed another day. Don't let this one pass by. Listen to your heart. It won't lead you wrong."

Jaime

"No, I understand. Thank you." Jaime took a shaky breath. "Yes, I'll be there tomorrow morning at nine."

Day four and only one of the eggs was viable. *Shit*.

She was staring at the screen of her phone when it rang in her hand, startling her so she jumped. The display said, *Connor calling*. Glancing at the time, she saw it was just after two. Too early for school to be out. He'd called every evening this week, just checking on her, but that was normally between the end of school and beginning of his high school practice. He made her think, and laugh, and after they hung up, she'd catch herself sighing and staring at the phone, wishing they'd had longer to talk.

Wondering what he wanted, she slid her thumb across the screen, accepting the call. "Hey, Connor."

"Jaime, you okay?" The concern in his voice was surprising, and his tone was warm and tender, like he had been the night of the procedure.

Taking a guess, she asked, "Marie got a call, too?"

She heard him blow out a hard breath, then he said softly, "Yeah."

"Is she okay? They said one was still dividing, so I'm going in the morning in case it's still cooking along." She swallowed. "I hate that the others didn't work."

"You do realize that nobody's going to be upset at you, right?" He sounded frustrated now. She knew he was busy. "Jaim?"

"I know. And I'm okay. I'll be there in the morning with high hopes in my heart."

Clearly her tone didn't fool him, because Connor said, "I'm on my way to your place already, should be there in five minutes. Want me to pick up anything?"

Jaime looked around at the tables, books, stacks, and other patrons, a big grin on her face. "I'm...uh...not home."

"Where are you?" Now he sounded super frustrated, and if he'd left his job so he could come console his brother's surrogate, she wasn't surprised he'd be irritated. Then the idea that he would be driven to console his brother's surrogate echoed in her head, and she blinked furiously. *That's all I am*, she reminded herself. Connor interrupted her thoughts, saying, "I'll come to you."

"I'm just getting a couple of things for Nate." She nodded at the volunteer as she took her card back and slid the resource books across the counter. Nate had reserved several last week. She put them into her bag, stacking them in one at a time. Surprised at the weight, she grunted when she picked it up. The books were heavier than she expected.

"What was that? Are you okay?"

"Connor." She laughed at his tone, filled with an unaccustomed concern. "I've fully recovered. I'm just at the library. Nate needed some books for homework this week."

"Are you at Hooks? That's even closer. I'm on Union now." He sounded distracted and she heard a car's horn through the phone. "Just turned onto Poplar. Wait for me."

"There's a bus stop literally right outside, Connor." She couldn't deny that she wanted to see him again. She knew she'd slept through much of the time he'd been with her Monday, but after she ate the soup, the three of them had played card games, laughing and chatting until it was Nate's bedtime. Now it was Friday, and he said he was coming to her. "But if you were seriously close by, I wouldn't turn down a ride. These books are heavy."

He chuckled, and she smiled at the sound. "I'll be in the parking lot when you get out there. Want me to stay on the phone?"

Rolling her eyes, she shook her head. "I think I can walk outside by myself. See you in a couple of minutes, Connor."

"Turning the corner now. Walk fast, Jaim." With that, the call disconnected and she blew out the breath that had gotten stuck in her chest at the soft, intimate tone his voice had taken there at the end. *All in your mind, woman.*

By the time she made it to the parking lot, he was out of the truck and leaning against the fender on the passenger side. Bare arms crossed on his chest, his boots were firmly planted on the asphalt. She did a double take. *Boots.* Puzzled, she took in his clothing as she approached. Jeans, western belt, cowboy boots, and a T-shirt didn't scream teacher and coach. "Hey, Connor. You taking the day off?"

He nodded as he reached out to take the bag and she was somewhat piqued when he lifted it off her already aching shoulder without any effort. *It's heavy, dang it.*

"Yeah, I spent the morning helping my dad with some equipment on the farm." One hand holding the truck door open for her, he waited until she was settled to place the bag of books by her feet. "I'd planned to make it back in time for lunch, was going to call you and see if you wanted to join me." *Not a date*, she told herself, listening to him and thinking, *Just two people who needed to eat.* "Then Coop called and I decided the joining was no longer optional." He leaned across her and she heard the click of her seatbelt, realizing he had just buckled her into the truck while she stared at him with her mouth open. "Lucky for me, I was right here. And here you are." He stayed close, face near hers when he asked, "You okay?"

She pressed her lips together for a moment before answering, then told him honestly. "I'm sad. I'm afraid that I'll get there tomorrow and they'll tell me we need to start the cycle again. I want this for Marie and Cooper, so I'm sad for them, not me."

He didn't move, and she had an up-close view of how his already dark brown eyes grew hooded when he looked at her mouth. "It'll be okay." His gaze traveled up her face until it reached her eyes, then he said, "We do another cycle, I'll be there with you. It'll be okay."

The concentration with which he stared at her was unnerving. Terrifying. As if he saw past the person she let everyone else see, and inside *her*. She cast around for something to say, running his words back through her head, trying to find something not terrifying to catch hold of. "So…lunch?" *Book fumes in the library must have made me stupid*. "I mean, you haven't had lunch yet? It's late."

Connor blinked, and when his eyes opened again, the intensity was dialed back. Not gone, but subdued, as if he realized how he'd frightened her with his words and gaze. Instead of answering her, he asked his own question. "What time does Nate's school let out?" He stepped away, saying, "Hold that thought." He shut her door and quickly rounded the hood of the truck, then climbed in beside her. "What time?"

"He gets home just after three." She pulled out her phone to look at the time. "I've got plenty of time to get home, especially if I'm not taking the bus."

"What time does he get out of class?" Truck started, Connor then pulled onto the road, traveling away from her apartment and towards Nate's school.

"Two thirty. Why?" She twisted to look behind them. "This is the wrong way."

"We can pick up Nate and do dinner instead." Connor stated this as if it were a given, something she should have already known.

"What?" *Why am I always confused around him?* "I can't do dinner."

"What?" Now he was the one sounding confused. "Why?" His voice dropped an octave, and carried a menacing growl when he asked, "Do you have a date?"

"What? No!" She pressed her palms against her cheeks, huffing out a breath. "Let's back up a minute to where I was at the library and had my whole day planned out. That's where I am. I can't seem to keep up, Connor. Tell me what you're doing here."

"I wanted to take you out to eat. I'm too late for lunch, so I figured we'd do dinner. I know you have Nate, and if we pick him up, we can all sit down together." Stated like that, it sounded so plausible, she found herself nodding along with him.

"He'll have homework." Connor made a turn, then another one and she realized even if she hadn't told him what school Nate went to, he was driving directly towards the campus. "How do you know where we're going?"

"Nate told me." Connor glanced at her for a long moment, then faced front, turning on the blinker and steering the truck into a parking lot. He glided the vehicle to a halt and put the transmission in park, then turned to her. With one arm propped on the steering wheel and one on the back of the seat, it seemed like he took up a lot of room and she found herself moving back from him. They stared at each other for a moment, then he pulled in a deep breath.

"Here's where I am, Jaime. When I saw you at Nate's first practice, I liked you." One corner of his mouth quirked up. "I surely liked what I saw. Liked how you were with your boy, and your spunk when you talked to me." His tongue slipped out, trailing across his bottom lip. "Nothing about you was lost on me, and I *liked* what I saw." The emphasis was unmistakable, and Jaime felt a blush begin to creep up her neck to her cheeks.

Connor shook his head. "Then, when I found out who you were, I was prepared to not like you. I don't have a reason. I'm an asshole sometimes." He snorted. "Marie'd tell you I'm stupid, too. I was prepared to not like you, but I couldn't unlike you." He kept his gaze on her, steady and weighted with an emotion she didn't understand. "I thought about you all the time. Wondering how you were dealing with everything. I knew parts of what was going on in your life, and that bugged me. After meeting you, I hoped I'd see you at the clinic and in preparation for that, I talked to Coop. That's when I found out Marie liked you. She thinks if you two had met somewhere in the natural course of life, you'd be friends. Like your friendship is bigger than the surrogate thing. I like that she likes you, because I like Marie. She's the little sister I never had."

She wanted to be able to look at him without craning her neck, so she unbuckled and turned to face him. When she moved, he paused talking for a moment and shifted in the seat, but other than a quick flick down and up her body, his gaze didn't stray from her face. This meant something to him. Something beyond what she understood. "Monday, at the clinic I got handed a chance at being something you needed. I didn't turn that chance down. I wanted to get to know you, to see if there was something under the *you* I liked. And there is, Jaime. There's more to like."

He shook his head. "I can't explain what's in my head right now. I just know, with my whole heart, that I want to get to know you better. I can't say I've ever felt that way about a woman before. This feels fast. Fuck, this feels like I'm in hyperdrive. That's one of the reasons I went out to help Dad today. He's got a way of talking through the bullshit. I laid it out for him, because me liking my brother's surrogate is not something I expected. Wanna know what he told me?"

She nodded, waiting. Everything he had said so far hadn't made her more scared; instead, it settled her. Knowing he felt the same connection she did was comforting. *I'm not in this alone.*

"Listen to your heart." Connor shook his head. "My old man's smart. Jaime, my heart says I want to get to know you. Today. I don't want to wait. I'm not a kid and I might coach there, but this isn't high school, I'm not into playing games. I like you. I wanted to have lunch, but then it took longer to get his tractor's PTO reassembled, which leaves the option of dinner." He paused and took a breath. "Would you go to dinner with me?" He smiled crookedly. "Fair warning, I'm not taking no for an answer."

"Can we eat at home? Nate will have homework." He smiled at her quickly stated willingness to acquiesce, and looked like the cat that got the cream.

"It's Friday. He's got all weekend to do his homework."

She shook her head. "I have to be at the clinic early in the morning, and since it's a weekend, he'll have to go with me. Then tomorrow afternoon is basketball. That only leaves Sunday, and I try to make sure he does something age-appropriate at least once a week. Sunday is blanket forts and movies day. The normal homework doesn't take him any time to complete, but his tutor challenges him. That's Mr. Paterson. He's the principal, and he's the one who insisted on the testing. He knows what Nate is capable of, or will be capable of, as long as we keep him focused. So tonight is homework."

With a smile, Connor leaned over and shoved at her leg with his palm, moving her so she faced the windshield of the truck. A moment later and she felt the heat from his body all along her front as he stretched, leaning across her for the seatbelt buckle. His mouth was inches from hers while he tugged and clicked it into place. "Gotta keep you safe," he murmured, puffs of air from his mouth ghosting across her lips. Then Connor did the same slow blink he'd done before and pulled back to refasten his own seatbelt. Pulling out of the parking lot, he said, "So you don't mind the meal, just the location. You need to go back to the apartment to pick up anything for him to do his homework?"

"No, why?" Her head was still spinning from everything he had said. All of it, and the implications were stupefying.

"Let's negotiate. You vetoed a dinner out, so we'll do barbecue and slaw in." He glanced at her with a sly smile. "At my house."

"No can do." She smiled as she denied him even this, lessening the sting with her reasons. "My apartment, so when it's bedtime, I don't have to get on a bus with Nate."

Connor

How in the hell did I not know what I've been missing? He glanced down at his leg, already wishing for a return of the heat from Nate's head as he lay on the couch between Connor and his mother. The kid had dozed off with his head resting on Connor's lap, feet tucked into Jaime's. Connor glanced up at the apartment building again and pulled out of the parking lot. Tomorrow was Saturday, and if he didn't make a reason to see her before, he'd at least get to see her at basketball. *That's fifteen hours away*, his brain complained, and Connor snorted a laugh at his impatience, knowing the single kiss he'd stolen would have to do until then.

Cupping her face in his hands, Connor drifted his thumbs across her cheeks in a slow caress. Bending close, he watched her tongue trace along her bottom lip, knowing the movement telegraphed her nervousness. "I'm just gonna kiss you," he whispered and saw her pupils dilate. They were standing near the door and he'd led her there by the hand, unwilling to put any distance between them. Her lips parted to respond as he slanted his mouth over hers, her head angling instinctively to allow him the kiss he'd demanded. Slow and steady, he brushed across side-to-side, building the intensity with each motion. She met him eagerly, every response pushing them forwards and as his breathing grew ragged he realized he had to slow things down. Pressing his forehead against hers, he kissed her softly, more a purse of the lips than anything else. "Night, Jaime," he whispered.

Dinner had been a hit with Nate, as had being picked up from school. His relief at not riding the bus seemed deeper than Connor would expect, and he wondered what was going on there. It wouldn't take much for kids to find something to pick at, and by leaving campus for half the day to go to the high school, Nate had enough different about him that he'd be a prime target. Connor reminded himself to e-mail Miles on Monday to see if there was anything going on, glad his buddy was the PE teacher for the grade school.

He steered the truck towards Cooper's house, needing to talk to his brother. First his father, now Cooper. He grinned. *Maybe I am in high school after all.* Homework had been an eye-opening exercise. Hearing

Jaime talk about Nate's intelligence and even talking to him was one thing. Seeing it in action, an entirely different experience. He seemed to remember almost everything he'd read, and she wasn't kidding when she said the "normal" homework went fast. Kid was so smart Connor was surprised rumors about him hadn't reached the school where he taught.

Pulling into Cooper's driveway, he put the truck in park and sat a minute. The grade school Nate attended wasn't the best. The high school was better, but the only reason it was a fit for him was the principal. *Where I work would be a good fit, too*. He'd quizzed her about it, so Connor knew the apartment Jaime would be moving to was in the same school district. It was another low-rent place, with a revolving door of tenants, which was why she'd been able to secure another apartment so quickly. *Wonder if I can call Paterson, see what he thinks about transferring Nate to my school*. He shook his head. That would be a no-go he knew, even without talking to Jaime. The apartments near where he worked cost triple of the rent the ones Jaime was looking at. *They could live with—*

He didn't finish the thought, rearing back in the seat and holding onto the wheel with stiff arms, as if he were bracing for a head-on collision. *Jesus Christ. Faster than hyperdrive*.

Swinging out of the vehicle, he jogged up the steps and knocked softly, eschewing the doorbell. It was that weird time of night when it wasn't early enough to be certain they'd be awake, but not late enough to think

109

they'd be in bed. He did know that Sam would be asleep already, like Nate, and didn't want to wake his nephew.

Nate had made no bones about the fact he liked Connor being at their place tonight. From the instant Jaime had walked out of the school with him beside her, the kid had been attentive and solicitous. He climbed into the backseat and buckled without being asked, then quickly agreed to every suggested dinner option. After breezing through homework and food, he had swiftly cleaned the table, stacking dishes in the dishwasher. While it was clear this was his assigned chore, the speed had surprised Jaime, and that made Connor laugh. Nate's offer to go hang in his bedroom had stripped the smile from her face, though, and her refusal hadn't allowed argument. That was when Connor had realized they wouldn't have any privacy otherwise, and had to hide a grin as he understood what the kid had been doing.

The door in front of Connor opened, and he stared down at Cooper's flushed face. Wet hair stuck up all over his head and he had a towel wrapped around his waist. "Is everything okay?" The barked question was a surprise until Connor looked beyond Cooper to see Marie walking down the stairs, towel wrapped around her hair.

"Oh, shit, bro. Sorry, man." Clearly he'd interrupted shower sex, and he flinched at the thought. "I can go." He took a step back, stopping when Marie held up a hand.

"Too late to retreat, Con. I'll go rustle up some coffee." She turned and headed into the kitchen.

He called after her, "Make it a beer. I need sleep." She made a sound he took as agreement.

Cooper reached out and grabbed his shirt, dragging him inside. "Get in here and tell me if Jaime's okay so I can go get dressed."

"Yeah, she's fine. She'll be at the clinic in the morning, ready if the egg is viable." He shook his head, softly closing the door. "I didn't mean to interrupt, Coop. I just wanted to talk to you if you were still up."

"Oh, I was up all right." Cooper was grinning now, and Connor faked a shiver.

"Don't say shit like that. Marie's like my sister. I do not need to think about what kind of freaky shit the two of you do in the shower." Connor eyed his brother. "Get some clothes on. I also don't need the scarring I'd take if you happened to slip up and drop the towel. I'll be in the kitchen."

Laughing, Cooper ran up the stairs as Connor walked in to see Marie standing with two beers at the kitchen island. He lifted one brow in a silent question, and she smiled. "I'm going to bed. It was a long day." Pursing his lips, he didn't say anything, just made his way over and pulled her into a tight hug. Marie whispered, "She's okay?"

"Yeah. How'd you know I would have talked to her?" He was puzzled, because he hadn't talked to or seen Marie and Cooper since he left the clinic with Jaime on Monday. "What gave you that idea?"

"Your daddy called today. Seems he's convinced his baby boy, who he's been worried about since Cole died, has found 'the one.'" Her arms came out to the sides and she made air quotes with her fingers when she said "the one," which made him laugh. "It didn't take a lot of deduction on our part. Not after seeing how you were with her at the clinic. Coop said you're coaching her son?"

Resting his chin on Marie's head, he nodded, knowing she'd feel the movement. "He's something else, Marie." Connor swallowed and licked his lips, aware he was about to admit to something that might not be well received. "She's...it's hard to explain. When I saw her, I thought she was cute. Pretty. Then she got sassy, and that was cute, too. Cuter. Then she shut down and I didn't get it right away. I liked what I saw, and she did too, so why would she slam the door? Then I saw her with Nate and I got it. I was her boy's coach, and she wouldn't mess that up for him by going after what she wanted. Such a mom thing, you know?" Marie hummed in agreement. "Then I figured out who she was and I was glad she'd closed down. But pissed. Man, I was pissed. It felt like I'd had something ripped away. Like I was missing something I didn't know I needed. I'm struggling, Marie. You think it's weird?"

Muffled against his chest, Marie said, "I'll be honest. I really did. I mean, finding a woman you like? Con, you know I'm over the moon for you. But for her to be our surrogate? That's just slightly strange. It doesn't feel wrong, just off. Or it did. That was before I peeked into recovery and saw you with her." She pushed at his chest and he relaxed his arms, letting her pull away. Marie took a step backwards and looked up into his face just as Cooper came into the room. "It's still slightly strange, but the heart knows what it wants."

Leaning into him, she placed a palm on his sternum, pressing hard. "Your heart has been hurting for a long time, Connor." He gritted his teeth against a sudden need to interrupt her, stop whatever she was going to say. "You and Cole had an amazing connection. Two brothers who always knew what the other was going to say, what they felt, what they were doing. That was ripped away from you and everyone who loves you sees how that hurts. We miss him in our lives, but you miss him *in* you. If Jaime is the one who can heal you, make your heart whole again, then don't let something stupid like her being our surrogate stop you."

She glanced at Cooper, then back to Connor. "We were talking earlier that maybe the eggs not being viable is a blessing. We can get another surrogate and then that leaves the field wide open for you and her." He opened his mouth and she silenced him with a wave. "Whatever happens, don't let it stop you from going after what you want. If she makes your heart whole, then don't let her get away. Finding people to love isn't easy, but we all know that life isn't easy." Tears quivered on her lower lids and she blinked them away. "Do what feels right. Your heart won't accept anything less than perfect, so if it's leading you to her, then follow."

Slowly Connor nodded. "Thanks, little sis."

"No prob, Connor. I love you." Cooper stepped behind her and wrapped his arms around her. She rested her hands on his where they crossed her chest. "We love you."

"Jesus, I'm glad I missed this convo if it wound up in the sappy stuff." Cooper grinned and bussed his wife's cheek loudly. "That beer for me?"

She twisted in his arms and scowled at him, then patted his cheek before pulling away. "You're a master at breaking the mood, husband. See you, Con."

Connor called, "Thought mood wrecking was my domain?" Marie's laughter trailed after her.

They waited until her footsteps reached the bedroom overhead before either spoke. Cooper asked, "You good now?"

"Dad called, huh?" Connor laughed, grabbing the open beer Marie had left on the counter for him as Cooper nodded. "Yeah, I'm good. Your wife's kinda smart."

"She is that."

Jaime

"Not viable," she repeated the tech's words flatly.

"No, the last egg stopped at some point last night. The doctor will be in to see you in a few minutes." The tech paused and said softly, "It's not the end of the process. We'll do another cycle and see what happens." Fiddling with the items she'd brought in on the small tray, the tech looked up at Jaime. "If you want to continue, I've got the shot right here."

Jaime nodded and stood, turning and pulling down the waistband of her jeans. "It's not something I did? Not something wrong with me?"

"Not at all." A pause, then the tech swiped her cheek with the alcohol swab. "Little stick, little burn. You know the drill."

Jaime pulled in a breath and said firmly, "I do."

Twenty minutes later she and Nate were sitting on the bench at the bus stop, and she was going over the paperwork again. She folded the sheets and pushed them into her bag before slinging it over her shoulder. Nate had been quiet since leaving the clinic, but he leaned into her now and asked, "You okay, Mom?"

"I am. I don't know why I'm so disappointed. But I'm perfectly all right." She glanced at her phone. "We've a while before the bus. What do you wanna talk about today?" That was their thing: Nate would pick a topic and he'd answer while she asked twenty questions, grilling him on the topic, often without her knowing a thing about whatever he was talking about. Her questions would sometimes send him into gales of laughter, which was why she was always willing to play their game. Those dimples would pop out and she'd grin right back at him, missing Brice the whole time.

"Coach T." Her chin came up and she twisted to look at him. "He likes you, Mom."

"Pick a different topic." She shook her head. "Off limits." Those were the rules. If she deemed the topic too mature or difficult, she would call a halt and he would pick a different subject.

"He likes you, Mom." Nate persisted, and she felt her face contorting into a scowl. He held up his palms. "Okay, how about 3D photography applications in the space program?"

Rolling her eyes, Jaime let her head fall backwards so she was staring through the clear Plexiglas ceiling of the bus stop. "3D photography in space. Okay. I got this." She closed her eyes but left her head tipped back. "What challenges are there in deploying 3D cameras in space?" She heard an engine stop nearby, but it was too early for the bus, so she didn't move. "That's question one. Question two is what benefit would there be in making 3D images of planets and things?" Some of his topics were easy, this one would be tough. "Question three, and then I'll have to think of others while you answer. Question three is which country would most leverage the information of 3D photography of the earth?"

"Oh, good questions, Mom." Nate sounded excited and that made her smile.

"Yeah, good questions, Mom." That was Connor's voice, and she snapped her head up, twisting to look to the side. He stood there, grinning down at her. "Hold that thought, buddy. Come on, Jaime." He stretched out his hand and waited patiently.

"Where are we going?" She placed her palm in his, and he gave a tug, pulling her up and off the bench, and against his chest.

"Breakfast." Nate whooped at the word, and she tilted to look around Connor at her son who was grinning up at her.

"We had breakfast," she reminded Nate, and he shook his head. "Yes, we did."

"Three hours ago, Mom. I'm hungry." He grabbed his backpack and turned, running towards the truck parked in the clinic's lot. The lights on the truck blinked and he yelled over his shoulder, "Thanks, Coach."

"Kids are always hungry," Connor said, and she tilted back, looking up at him. His face softened when he said, "Hi, Jaime."

Last night had been wonderful. He had been attentive and sweet. Had seemed to understand exactly the kind of encouragement Nate needed, and had pitched in to help check some of the math work that could frustrate her. He had even seemed content to sit on the couch without touching, Nate stretched out between them, connecting them in a way that was sweet and so beautiful. How she'd always imagined things would have been if Brice lived. *Brice didn't live*, she reminded herself. *But Connor's right here*.

"Hi, Connor. You don't have to feed us. You paid for dinner just last night." One corner of his mouth quirked up. A thought struck her. "Plus, don't you have to get ready for basketball?" He pursed his lips and shook his head. "Oh, no, is basketball canceled today? Nate will be disappointed."

"Practice is still on, Jaime. But I don't have to do a ton of preparation for a weekly program. That's all laid out before we begin. Plus, if I decided to play hooky today, my assistants would fill in. I know when we had dinner, and I also know I had the most fun and relaxing evening I've had in a while. Slept really well. Overslept, in fact, because I'd intended to be here to go in with you if you wanted. Or I'd have hung with Nate in the waiting room." He leaned down, getting close and she was suddenly glad his frame blocked Nate's view from the truck, because he brushed his mouth across hers. Pulling back slightly, he was still close enough his breath caressed her lips when he whispered, "Hyperdrive. I'm going full steam ahead until you pull the brakes." Angling in, he kissed her again, then whispered, "You want to pull the brakes, Jaim?"

Eyes open through both kisses, brief as they were, she stared into his deep brown eyes and shook her head. "No," she said, the movement accompanying the word causing her lips to graze across his. His eyes darkened, growing impossibly black. His hand wrapped around her neck, bringing her that fraction of an inch closer until he was kissing her again, softly, questing side to side in a gentle caress.

Pulling back again, he straightened, gaze locked with hers and told her, "Good."

Breakfast turned into video games at the arcade, and then lunch. It was almost two before he walked Jaime and Nate up to their apartment. Jaime shivered when she saw Solon in the doorway to the office, feeling his gaze on her like a greasy touch. Connor had his arm around her and must have felt her reaction, because he asked, "Who's the douche?"

Fortunately, Nate was already racing up the stairs and didn't hear him, so Jaime answered, "Apartment manager. I'll be glad to get out of here." She thought about the pile of boxes still needing to be assembled and taped, then filled and carried on the bus. They didn't have that much to move, but it would still take her several trips.

"When are you planning to move?" Connor's neck stayed twisted as he glared over his shoulder at Solon, and she giggled at the protective move. "What?" He looked at her.

"Nothing. I'll probably start moving Wednesday. Maybe finish up on Thursday." She shrugged, liking the heat of his arm where it lay across her shoulders. "Not much to pack up. Furniture all stays."

"Why will it take you two days, then?" They were headed up the stairs, and he shifted his hold, moving to grip her hand instead. "You got stuff in storage?"

Shaking her head, she huffed a laugh. "No, just takes a while to move."

He slowed when they reached the landing before her floor, pulling her to a halt with his hold on her hand. "What's the problem, Jaime?"

"No problems. I'll do a few loads over on Wednesday while Nate's in school, see how close I can get to being done. Then if I finish on Thursday, I'll meet him back here and we'll bus over." She shook her head, digging in her pocket for her keys, heading towards the remaining flight of stairs. "I don't think he has his keys with him. I need to unlock the apartment."

"A few loads?" He took two stair treads to her one, and somehow they still managed to reach the top together.

"On the bus," she said, seeing she was wrong because Nate was missing but the apartment door was open. She squeaked when Connor abruptly stopped, turning her to face him. He looked puzzled, and maybe slightly pissed. "Connor?"

"You're moving, you rent a truck. If you don't rent a truck, you rent a van. If you have a friend with a truck—" He lifted his other hand, hooking a thumb at himself. "—you ask that friend if they can help." He folded his fingers into his hand, rubbing his knuckles across his chest, a movement she'd seen him do before. It looked painful, but he didn't even seem to notice he was doing it. "Jaime. Why didn't you say anything?"

"I didn't think about it, Con. I was already planning the move before"—she gestured between them—"this happened. I didn't mean to slight you."

Narrowing his eyes, he stared down at her, then broke into a broad grin. "I've got a lot of vacation time because I do clinics during the summer and breaks." She shook her head and shrugged, not understanding. He leaned in and kissed her softly. "Looks like I'll be using one of those vacation days on Wednesday."

Connor

"You movin' the bitch?" The question was so unexpected Connor missed the first step on the staircase, thumping his shin painfully against the edge of the tread. He turned to see the sleazy manager leaning against the hallway between the office and where Connor stood. "'Bout time she got her ass in gear and got out the fuckin' door."

Connor took a moment to study the man. Tall and thin, he looked like he spent his days inside a tiny room, never seeing the outdoors. Tipping his head back slightly, the man tried to stare him down. "Miss Grimes is moving today, yes." Connor shifted, adjusting to balance on the balls of his feet. "She'll mail in the keys."

"Save her the postage, follow you up." The man turned his head, and Connor wouldn't have been surprised if he'd spit on the floor. Connor didn't try to hide the disgust he felt and didn't care that it showed when the man looked at him again. "You tappin' that ass?"

Connor glanced down at himself, taking stock. Jeans and a button-down shirt, the guy probably thought he'd be an easy target to intimidate. *Think again, asshole.* Lifting his chin, he stared at the manager, taking a step closer, crowding into his space. "Here's how this is gonna go. You're gonna turn your ass around and head to your office. You're not going to speak to me again. You're not going to speak to my girl. You're going to keep your fap dreams to yourself, and lose the fuckin' attitude you copped because she didn't have the time of day for a fuckin' loser like you. I'm headed up, and when I come back down with the first load of boxes, you need to be absent. That means—" He tilted his head, not looking away from the man's face. "—that you need to not fuckin' be where I can see you. I'm not what you think, asshole. And you—" Connor let his gaze flicker down and up. "—ain't anything I'm worried about."

Without another word, Connor turned and went up the stairs, two at a time, trying to burn off the anger roaring through him at the idea of Jaime having to deal with that fucker for however long she'd lived here.

Outside her door, he took a minute, taking deliberate deep breaths, reminding himself of every reason he could think of to not go back downstairs and beat the shit out of that ass. *I just want to take care of her, take care of them both.* At least the asshole on the bus had been handled for Nate. *Getting a reaction out of a school administrator is easier when you're the teacher,* he thought. Thankfully it was a moot point now, since Nate would be on a different bus route coming from school to the new apartment.

Lifting a hand, he rapped the backs of his knuckles sharply against the door. Footsteps approached and a moment later he heard the chain being taken off. Then the door opened and Jaime stood there. More beautiful than she'd been last night, more beautiful than any woman he'd ever seen. He held her gaze as he leaned in, losing her eyes at the last second when she let them dip closed, her dark blonde lashes touching her cheeks as he brushed his lips across hers. She made a throaty sound, a cross between a gasp and a moan, and he deepened the kiss, tracing the seam of her mouth with his tongue, diving inside when she opened to him.

Stepping close, he swept his arms around her and crushed her to his chest, holding her tight as he slanted his head, working his mouth across hers again and again. She was trembling when he broke away, realizing he was calculating the amount of time it would take to get her undressed and to the couch. "We can't," he said, feeling his voice rip up his throat.

"No." She buried her face against his chest, fingers fisted in his shirt that had somehow become unbuttoned. She choked off a laugh, telling him, "Not a problem I expected to have."

He kissed the side of her head softly, smiling. "Me, either."

Abstinence. Demanded of the donors, and hers was the more critical of the two, at least for the delicate period before a positive pregnancy test.

"I'll do my best to keep a handle on it from here out." He smiled when she groaned. "You got boxes packed?" Without picking her head up, she nodded, rocking her forehead against the bare skin of his chest. The brush of her hair on his skin was torture. "I should get to hauling them downstairs then. Sooner we get done, the sooner this place is in your rearview mirror."

Jaime

"Nate'll take the new bus here after school. I called and talked to Mr. Paterson to make sure. I think that makes it official. We're moved in." Jaime stood in the kitchen, unpacking the last box, arranging the serving spoons and utensils in the drawers.

"Okay." Connor's voice was closer than she expected. When she looked up, he was only a few feet behind her, a puzzling expression on his face.

"What?" He'd been finishing up with Nate's things, arranging the books on a set of shelves they'd moved from the living area into his bedroom.

"You"—he moved closer—"have a bedroom now." Connor held out one hand and took the box she'd just unpacked, making quick work out of breaking it down before he tossed it on the floor to one side. "I just realized that."

"I do." Jaime dropped her gaze, suddenly unsure of herself. *God, I don't know what to do with my eyes, so*

what am I going to do with my hands if it comes to that?
"But, the clinic—"

"I know," he said, moving closer. He lifted one hand and traced along her eyebrow with a fingertip, making her shiver. "Nothing we can do about that part. But—" He lifted his other hand, applying pressure along the edge of her jaw, and she lifted her chin for him. "—we can do lots of other things." He dipped his head, and she felt the heat of his breath across her mouth. "Like this." The kiss started slow and gentle, more of an exploration than a possession, and she swayed towards him. "And this." He'd pulled back the tiniest amount and now skimmed his lips along her jaw, finding her earlobe with his teeth, nibbling and sucking on the sensitive flesh. "With you," he whispered, sliding his cheek along hers, "I'm up for anything you're interested in, Jaime."

"Nate—" she began, but he was there before she could finish her thought.

"Has a bedtime." When he pulled back to look down at her, the smile he flashed her was knowing and naughty. "We'll do homework, then dinner, then whatever the two of you want to do. And then, he'll go to bed."

"First night in a new place. He might be nervous." She shook her head. This was a bad idea for so many reasons.

"He might not be." Leaning in, he nuzzled the soft skin behind her ear. Then he whispered, "Nothing to be worried about, Jaime. At this point, there are no wrong

125

answers to anything we do, or don't do, as long as we color within the lines. Be easy, honey. Be easy."

Seated on the couch after Nate made his way to bed, Jaime was cuddled into Connor's side. He had music playing on his phone, something soft and instrumental. The evening had gone amazingly. Nate was happy with his room and pleased with having Coach around another night. She'd cooked, and Connor had eaten two servings of her sausage potato bake, which had stroked her ego just enough. He didn't seem in a hurry to pick up where they'd left off in the afternoon, and she was content to sit here for as long as he was willing.

He shifted, and she changed positions slightly, relaxing against his side again. "Hey," he said softly. "Tell me about your brother."

"God, Jacob. That's a big topic. What do you want to know?" She couldn't remember what she'd told him about Jacob and didn't want to broach a sensitive subject like his sexuality if it would ruin the mood. That was why he'd had to move away from Memphis, after all.

"Tell me about growing up."

"Pitching me a softball, I like it. Thanks, Coach." Jaime tipped her chin up and Connor leaned down to give her a kiss, something he'd done at odd times all day. Something she liked. "We grew up in Memphis, but Jacob had a tough time of it. After high school, he got a scholarship to a California college. He's a graphic artist. Amazing artist, honestly. Every medium he uses, Jakey can produce breathtaking things."

"You call him Jakey? That's cute." Connor's arm tightened around her.

"He calls me James." She laughed. "I hated it growing up. Love it now."

"Cole called me Conman." She looked up in time to see the smile on his face fade away. "I called him Coleslaw, of course. Coop has always just been Coop."

"Kids." She said this like it didn't need explanation, and she supposed it didn't since he agreed with a laugh. "Nater Potater. Don't tell him I told you. It's something he outgrew a couple of years ago, but I'll slip up and say it sometimes." He laughed again, chest rumbling with the sound of his humor.

"I should go," he said, and she sighed. "I don't want to. I'll make that clear, Jaime."

"I don't want you to go. But, you have school tomorrow." Shaking her head, she said, "That sounds odd to say to a grown man. You have school."

"Only because you're a mother, and you're used to telling your nine-year-old the same thing." He moved, leaning in, and she lifted her chin, meeting his lips with hers. This time it was her tongue dipping into his mouth for a moment, until he chased it back into hers, groaning into her mouth. "I want to stay, Jaime." He shifted her and stood, drawing her to her feet. "So I'll promise you that one night soon," lips against hers, he whispered, "I will."

127

Chapter Ten
Connor

"You didn't see her the last time." Connor was on the phone with Cooper. Tomorrow Jaime would be undergoing the procedure again to collect the eggs. Connor would be at the clinic earlier this time, to do his part, then planned to stay with her, from beginning to end. "Did the clinic talk about the other method?"

"Intrauterine? Yeah, but there's less of a chance of success and a greater chance of multiples going directly into the uterus with the donor sperm. IVF is accepted as the best way to manage the process." Cooper had a patient tone in his voice that grated on Connor's nerves.

"Yeah, but you didn't see her puking her guts out for hours. So out of it from the anesthesia that she didn't even know I'd left until I got back, three hours later. Marie did, ask her. Coop, IUI works and it's not as traumatic." Connor raked his fingers through his hair, turning to look out the front window of his office and into the gym. "Fuck, man." He scanned the players working through drills, making a mental note to work with two of the juniors on making their passes snappy. "It's less expensive than in vitro, right?"

"Connor. I know you have a thing for Jaime right now—"

Connor cut him off. "It's not a thing. It's just…I like her, man. It killed me to see her like that and I barely knew her then. I know her now." He sighed, then growled out a rough, "*Fuck*." He forced himself to pull in another deep breath, then carefully said, "Sorry, Coop. I didn't mean to get in your business like that. I know Jaime's totally on board with whatever you've agreed to do. I'm on board, too. I just forgot for a minute what the end goal is."

"You really like her, don't you?" The surprise in Cooper's voice was clear, his voice warm. Happy. "It's not a quick thing. This really is it for you. She's it."

"Feels that way," Connor admitted. "Fast, so fucking fast I can't catch my breath, but I like her. I might love her, Coop. Her and Nate. He's amazing. I've never met a kid like him."

"Been spending some evenings over there I hear." Now Cooper's tone was sly, and Connor could envision the sideways grin on his face.

"Not like that. We play by the rules, man." That was the truth, but just thinking about their goodbye kiss last night had his cock straining at the front of his pants, threatening to tent them. "Hard as that's been."

"It's hard." Cooper snorted a laugh, and he and Connor finished the phrase together, something that had always made all three of the teenaged Thompson boys crack up. "So hard."

"Fuck you," Connor said, laughing. "See you in the morning, old man."

"You're not much younger than me. Better get your ass in gear, catch up on living." They disconnected and Connor stood, staring out the window to where his team was practicing, but he wasn't seeing two dozen sweaty teenaged boys. Instead, he remembered the flush on Jaime's face when he'd finished kissing her last night.

The past month had been hard on her. With Sam, Connor hadn't cared about the other parties involved. Had no idea how much commitment it took on the part of the donor. Daily shots, weekly visits, hell, Jaime had joked one evening it seemed like she spent half her time on her back. That hadn't sat well with Connor and he couldn't imagine how couples did this. If she hadn't already been invested in helping Cooper and Marie, he would definitely have tried to talk her out of it.

Last night had been...interesting. Connor had driven her to the clinic and then he and Nate sat in the waiting room chatting while she got her shot. On the way back to their apartment, Nate made a statement that shocked Connor. Shocked, and pissed him off.

"I remembered, Mom. I'll pick up all my homework for the rest of the week tomorrow." Connor met Nate's

eyes in the rearview mirror, seeing concern on the boy's features. "I explained and all the teachers were cool with it."

Jaime perked up, twisting in her seat to smile at her son in the backseat. "Perfect, Nate. Thank you."

"Why did you need to bring extra work home?" Connor looked away from Nate and to Jaime. "That's procedure day."

She nodded. "I've made arrangements to have someone bring me back to the apartment, and then Nate will stay with me. He's just being cautious and covering his bases in case I'm sick again." She smiled, leaning close and whispering, "He's a good kid."

"Nate is a good kid," he told her, pitching his voice low, but not trying to whisper. "But I'm going to be there. He can go to school."

"I'm staying home with Mom." Nate had clearly heard their conversation and was trying to put a stop to any chance of an argument. "You've got work, and I heard about the tournament. You'll be busy, Coach."

Connor stared out the window again. Nate had been right, of course. He was taking off tomorrow, which was Thursday, but Friday and Saturday he'd be tied up in the district basketball tournament. *Last time she was just sick the one day.* He shook his head, stomaching rolling. His hand lifted to his sternum, knuckles rubbing hard. Some of the material he'd been reading said it could last longer, though.

Chapter Eleven
Jaime

"I'm fine, Connor." She smiled up at him. He'd been hovering over her for the past thirty minutes while the tech started her IV and got the other monitoring hooked up. "In and out, half an hour, tops. Then once I can walk and talk—" The tech laughed and Jaime glanced in her direction with a grin on her face. "—then we can get out of here." It was strange how her nerves had calmed just because Connor was with her this time. *A lot has changed in just a month*.

He was frowning at her and she squeezed his hand, wrapping her fingers around his. "Promise, Connor. I'm fine."

"I'll be right here when you come out." He leaned down, getting close as he whispered, "See you on the other side, beautiful."

Regaining her senses in recovery seemed easier this time, and she was carried upwards on a swell of awareness by Connor talking to her. It didn't matter what he was saying, just knowing he was there like he'd promised was enough. She blinked and rolled her head to the side where he was sitting, seeing how he dwarfed the tiny recliner pulled close to her bed. "Hey, Jaime. There you are. How you feeling?"

She licked her lips and tried out her voice. "Good." She lifted a hand and scrubbed at her nose, careful of the needle in the back of her hand. "Pretty good. How many?" Letting her eyes close, she relaxed back into the bed. "Eggs, how many?"

"Seven, really good ones, too. Coop and Marie just left. She's over the moon." Jaime smiled, knowing that would be true. She and Marie had hoped for that many, or more. "They've already introduced them to their swimmers." Eyes still closed, she laughed at that. "So now, we wait." She fumbled in the covers, feeling around for the button on the cord she'd used last time. "What do you need, Jaime?"

"Call button." Instead of the hard, cold plastic, her hand encountered something warm that gently gripped her fingers. Connor's hand. "I'm thirsty."

"I'm right here, James." She heard the sound of water being poured into a glass, then paper tearing. "Open."

Obediently she opened her mouth and accepted the straw, wrapping her lips around it and taking a long drink of cold water. "Thanks," she said, finally opening her eyes again to see him staring at her mouth, a familiar expression of frustration on his face.

Guilt ripped at her, again, as it had every time she'd seen him over the past weeks. They were forced by circumstances to take it slower than some of the teenagers he taught. Connor had been so understanding it surprised her, but then he explained how his part required abstinence, too. Not for as long as she had to, but it at least gave him an empathy he might not have otherwise had.

This all meant kissing and touching had been all they'd done. Some good kisses. *Really good kisses*, she thought, lifting her fingertips to her lips. *Scorching hot kisses*. She lifted her gaze to meet his again and saw heat there to match her own. *Hormones*, she told herself for the thousandth time. *At least he's getting the full gamut of emotions from me; there won't be any surprises down the road*. The shots made her moody, and since she was horny too, it had seemed worse this time around.

"Killin' me," he groaned and leaned in, pressing his lips to hers in a hard, closed-mouth kiss. "More water?" She shook her head. "Anything else you want?" *You*, she thought, and he must have read it in her expression because he groaned again. "Swear, you'd never know what I was doing an hour ago."

That made her giggle, which was what the nurse heard when she walked in. "You sound chipper, Miss Grimes. About ready to blow this pop stand?" Detaching from all the medical equipment took a few minutes, as did the paperwork, then Jaime was walking out of the clinic leaning on Connor's arm.

Just like a month ago, but at the same time, so very different. So many changes in a month.

Connor

Sitting on the new couch in her new apartment, Connor looked down at the woman sleeping with her head on his leg. One hand tucked under his thigh, she was covered to her shoulders by the blanket Nate had brought her before he headed to bed.

Finally alone, Connor let himself remember what she'd told him in recovery.

"I'm falling in love with you."

It had felt like his heart had stopped in his chest, and he'd wondered for a moment what the monitors would show if he'd been hooked up to the machines instead of her. "I wanted you to know, honey." Jaime never used endearments, not with him. She called Nate baby and honey, and bud, but she'd always called him Connor.

He'd leaned down, getting close, not wanting to ask her anything because this wasn't fair, him being here and her being medicated gave him an unfair advantage. Holding his breath when her mouth opened again, her pink tongue trailing across the bottom lip. Was she talking to him, or Nate's dad? She had put any question to rest with her next words. "I'm falling in love with you, Connor Allen Thompson. And I'm scared of how I feel."

He'd whispered back to her, "Don't be scared, Jaime." After a glance at the monitors to confirm she was still sleeping, he'd confessed, "I'm falling in love with you, too."

Chapter Twelve

Jaime

"How many?" It was day four, and tomorrow would have her back in the clinic, if there were viable embryos. "How many are there?"

"We have four," Marie squealed in her ear. "Four developmentally competent embryos!"

"That's fantastic," Jaime told her, feeling like her smile could split her face. "How many are we going to implant?" This was something that the clinic had talked about a lot. Maybe even too much, as far as she was concerned. If it had been anyone other than Marie and Cooper, she would worry about the chance of having multiples, because the material had so strongly cautioned about the medical dangers. With Marie and Cooper? She wanted this for them enough to warrant the risks. "We going for all four?"

"No. Not a chance in hell, honey." Marie's words were firm. "Two, at the most. We'll freeze the other two, if we still have four in the morning."

"In the morning," Jaime whispered. "Are we really doing this?"

Marie's whisper was just as quiet as she answered, "We're really doing this."

Jaime pulled in a breath, then blew it out. "And this part is like super easy. Yay!"

"Yay!" Marie laughed, then said, "You haven't mentioned much about Connor. Is he being nice? I'll kick his ass if he's not. I've known him a long time, and I can tell you, he's not always nice."

"He's being super, really." Jaime angled her chin down, staring at her toes. "It feels surreal. I mean, I'd have met him anyway because of basketball. But to get to know him because of this? I keep waiting for it to feel too weird, but so far it's stayed just this side of strange."

"I'm glad, for both of you." Jaime laughed, and Marie insisted, "No really. I keep picturing you guys together in my head, and it works. He's been great through the whole process and is the best uncle my son could ever want. Connor hasn't had it too easy. When Cole was killed, it was like he went hollow. I mean, there were days when he'd show up at the farm and work, but you knew from the look on his face that if you asked him at the end of the day what he'd done, he couldn't have told you. I've been with Coop since he and I were fifteen, and I got to watch Cole and Con grow up. Those two were like peas in a pod, where you saw one you knew the other wasn't far behind.

Marie sighed. "The funeral, he sat and stared at the casket for the longest time. We had the visitation, and there were hundreds of people who had come to pay their respects. Connor didn't see them. He just...was lost. Not long after that he really threw himself into work. Summer clinics and conditioning camps, he taught all day and then worked with his kids at night. It was often weeks between times we'd see him. Coop missed him. It was like he'd lost both of his little brothers. Then we found out we couldn't have kids, you know all of that."

Jaime murmured softly, "Yeah. I know."

"Connor started talking to Coop about all kinds of avenues. Foster care was his first pitch, then he moved on to adoption. He's the reason we looked seriously at surrogacy. There was a show about it on TV. He came over and set-up a recording on our DVR." Marie snickered. "I'd never known he was squeamish, but he was over when we were watching it and they were talking about the birth process. He turned white, pale as a sheet."

Laughing, Jaime said, "Hard to believe big, strong Connor was floored by that."

"Yeah." Marie paused and sighed. "Tomorrow."

"Tomorrow," Jaime responded. "We're doing this."

They said their goodbyes and she disconnected the call, looking around the apartment. Furnished when they moved in, she and Nate had managed to put a tiny stamp of their personalities on the space with pictures on the wall, and favorite blankets folded on the back of the chair and couch. But there were bits of Connor, too. A pair of pants and a shirt she'd laundered yesterday, folded and on the table next to the door, there was a bag of his workout gear in her bedroom. He'd taken and printed a picture of the three of them sitting on a picnic table, eating ice cream, the selfie angled in such a way they all fit, and it was a close-up of their grinning faces. That was on the front of the fridge, held there by four magnets. She sighed, wondering if she liked seeing all of that too much. If this was too much, too fast, but he was always the one pushing for more.

Her phone buzzed and she glanced down, seeing a text from him. *Speak of the devil*, she thought, grinning.

Well?!??

She texted back a single number, knowing he'd understand. **4**

Awesome!

Yeah

You worried? Scared? Connor had been there every step of the way this cycle, but it still felt odd talking to him about things, knowing it would be his sperm that fertilized one of her eggs.

Not really. This is the easy part. :)

9am right?

Yeah. I'll go there after I get Nate to school. Geez, at this rate she could have called him and they could have talked through things faster. But he was teaching—she glanced at the clock—with only four minutes between gaggles of students in his room.

See you soon. We'll talk then. It was like he read her mind and she smiled again.

Okay.

I love you.

Whoa. That was unexpected, and she had a sudden vision of him shaking his head and cursing the phone, wishing he could take it back. There wasn't an undo button for text, though, and that one from him hung there in front of her, waiting for a response. Daring her to respond. Too fast. Way too fast.

Two options. Ignore it, and say she'd see him tomorrow night or the night after, or she could play it off as a joke.

Decided, she tapped in her response, checked it for errors, and hit send. No emoji, no over the top. Just an acknowledgment of what he'd texted, and a reassurance that if he really was there emotionally, she wasn't upset or put off by the declaration.

Awwww. You're in the fast lane today. I can't wait to see you.

She waited, and got no response, but could see he'd read her answer. She glanced at the clock again and realized his class would have already begun. She got up and moved around the apartment, straightening things, then ran downstairs to buy a paper. Once a week she looked through the want ads, hoping there'd be something that would fit her schedule. The bonus would be running out before she would be eligible for a payment from the clinic, and there was no way she'd risk having to move Nate again.

She was on the phone with an agency, going over their openings when her phone buzzed. After the call, she looked at the screen to see she had a new text from Connor. Opening the app, she read, **Cannot wait, gorgeous**.

"That's it?" Jaime asked as she smoothed her skirt down over her thighs. This had been more like a normal gynecologist appointment, and after the normal rounds of time consuming checks, she was a little surprised at the quickness of the procedure. "We're good?"

"Things look very good, Jaime," the doctor said, rolling towards her on the stool. Hands on her knees, he looked up at her. "There's good thickness in your lining, and we transferred the best two of the blastocysts. You'll have some instructions to review, but we're all systems go. No baths for a week, keep the stress levels low, and don't panic if there's a little light spotting. Now it's up to the embryos. If they implant, then we'll see a progression over the next couple of weeks." He patted her knees reassuringly, and stood, stepping back and helping her down from the table. "Call the office if you have questions. Otherwise, we'll see you in twelve days. The girls up front will make the appointment for you." He opened the door, preceding her into the hallway.

She turned towards the front office, and through the glass window into the waiting room, caught a glimpse of Connor. She slowed, watching as he flipped a page in the magazine in his hands, then angled his neck to look at the door leading to the back rooms. It was just after lunchtime, and he was supposed to be in school. In fact, she wasn't expecting to see him for a couple of days, because of his schedule and the team's games. Standing at the counter, she waited on the girl to hand her the appointment card with the day and time of her next visit, when they would do a pregnancy test. He looked up and saw her, a broad smile breaking across his face. "Hi," he mouthed, and she smiled back at him.

She opened the door and he was standing in front of her. "Hi," he repeated, and held out a hand towards the outside entrance. "I'm parked just outside."

"Connor, hi." She saw the nurse was waiting behind her, and politely stepped to one side, moving out of the doorway. "When did you get here? How...I thought you were working?"

"I was, but I wanted to be here. Wanted to see you." His hand dropped back to his side, and his shoulders straightened. His expression tightened and he looked tense, as if something was wrong. "I haven't been here long, but you didn't answer my text, so I figured you were still in the office."

143

She pulled her phone out and looked, two texts from him. "I was going to call Marie when I got home."

"Can I give you a ride? You can call her from the truck." Now he sounded less certain and she knew it was due to her reaction.

Jaime pulled in a breath. "Can I start over?" He stared at her a moment, then nodded. "I'm so glad to see you, Connor. I missed you." A look of relief rushed across his features, and he smiled when she finished with, "Thank you for coming."

"My pleasure, Jaime." He reached out and slipped his hand down her arm, threading his fingers through hers. "You ready to go?"

"I am."

In the truck, he turned towards her apartment while she texted Marie. After a few moments, he asked, "Hungry?"

Finishing up her text conversation with a reminder that they were now in the two-week window she'd taken to calling the cone of silence, Jaime did a quick calculation of her finances, reluctantly shaking her head. "I'll eat when I get home, thanks."

"So you are hungry?" His tone was playful, and she flashed him a grin as she tucked the phone into her pocket. "What do you want to eat, Jaime?"

"I'll just have something at home. I want to hang out on the couch until Nate gets home." She was turning to look out the window when she caught a glimpse of his expression. He looked almost pissed. "What?"

"We can pick up something and take it home." He reached out and captured her hand, resting their clasped hands on the seat between them. "Then you can hit the couch right away. You need to eat."

Embarrassed, she turned to stare out her window. "Connor—" she began, but he cut her off.

"How about I put it this way. I'm hungry, and I feel like having either a bucket of fried chicken or a bag of tacos and burritos. If you were willing to eat something from a drive-up place, which would you prefer? Or—" He squeezed her hand, and she looked at him. "—which would Nate like best?"

"He's a chicken kid, no doubt," she said before she thought, and then grimaced. Untangling her fingers from his, she started digging into her pocket for the little wallet she carried. "I don't have cash, but we can use my card to pay."

He didn't respond, just turned into the drive and pulled around to the speaker. "Anything Nate won't eat?"

"Connor—"

He cut her off again. "Not happening, Jaime." Connor flashed her a grin. "Lemme. Please?"

When they walked into the apartment, she was so exhausted all she wanted to do was curl up in a corner of

145

the couch and sleep. Yawning, she hooked one of the kitchen chairs out from under the table and sat, toeing off her shoes. "I'm just so tired." He carried the bag to the counter and pulled out plates. As if they did this every day. *Would that be so bad?* She caught her breath at the thought, then shook her head. Instead of saying anything like that, she asked, "Would you be offended if I napped?"

"Not a bit of it, Jaime. Why don't you try to eat a bite before you lie down?" He moved to the refrigerator and opened it, standing for a moment staring inside. "What do you want to drink?"

"Oh, just water." Jaime was conscious that the fridge was nearly bare. "I'm going shopping tomorrow. Grocery time." Laughing nervously, she bent over to pick up her shoes. "Seriously, I can't remember being this worn-out in a long time." Carrying her shoes, she put them on the rug next to the door and turned back, making her way across the small living room.

"You've had a lot going on." He turned from the counter and walked towards the couch, meeting her there and handing over one plate. "Eat up, then we'll nap."

We? Without answering him, she accepted the plate and sat on one end of the couch, propping her elbow and plate on the arm.

She was halfway through one of the pieces of chicken he'd put on her plate when he spoke. "Are we dating?"

Swallowing, she nodded. "Yes."

"If we're dating, then what am I?"

"You're Connor. What do you mean, what are you?" She was only now conscious of the weight in the room, the air seemed charged. They'd been quiet since sitting down, and she hadn't realized this was him stewing over something. He seemed tense and sat still, his jaw clenching repeatedly, a muscle in his cheek jumping.

"If I introduced you to a colleague, what word would I use? My girlfriend?" The words were clipped, harsh as he dropped them into the stilted silence between them. "My friend?"

That stung. He'd texted that he loved her, hadn't said the words yet, but she held that text close to her heart, and she didn't want to be his friend. "Your girlfriend?" *Dang.* She hadn't meant to sound so tentative, but that was how it came out.

"Yeah." He wasn't tentative. His words were firm, leaving no room for argument. "My girlfriend. And I'm your man. Your boyfriend. Your *partner.*"

"Okay?" Not sure what had prompted this conversation, she was treading carefully.

"You were surprised I was there today. And then you didn't want me to drive you home. And you sure didn't want me paying for a meal." He turned to look at her, and she saw his brows were drawn together, not in a scowl, but confused looking, hurt at something she'd

147

done. "Is that what you expect from me? To not be there, to not offer to assist, and to expect you to pay my way?"

"No." Bending, she placed the plate on the floor and turned to sit sideways on the couch, facing him. "I was surprised because I knew you had to work today. Teaching isn't factory work. They can't just call someone in to pull your lever for ten hours a day if you don't show up. It wasn't that I didn't want you there, or didn't want you to drive me home. I wasn't expecting to see you is all. And the food?" She shook her head. "I was just going to make a cup of soup or something when I got home. I didn't think about you being hungry, too. It was after lunch, so if I'd thought about it, I still would have expected you to have already eaten." She paused, tipping her head to the side to consider his expression, which had gone from pained and stormy, to thoughtful. "I'm sorry if I broke some girlfriend rule. I haven't done this in a very long time. You're going to have to cut me some slack sometimes."

"No, I'm sorry. I didn't think. I got up this morning and wanted to see you. I got to the school and there was a substitute in the lounge. He was there for another teacher's morning classes, but I got to thinking he could sub in for me the last two periods. Today was a big day, and I didn't want you to do it alone." Chin down, he stared at the plate on his lap. "I worked through lunch to throw together class plans that would make sense to him." He turned and looked at her, one side of his lips quirking. "I missed you."

"Connor." She paused, again choosing her words carefully. "You realize I'm not a...something to fix, right?" She'd barely avoided the word "problem," which she thought would probably make him angry. "I've been on my own a long time, and I'm used to dealing with things alone." He opened his mouth and she put him off with a raised palm. "I'm not saying I don't appreciate all the things you do for me. I do, honey. Like coming to the clinic today. That was incredibly sweet, and it makes me very happy that you want to be there with me. I want you there, too. But, we're both grown-ups. You said once this wasn't high school, and you're right. It's not. You've got a job, and I've got a child. I don't expect you to take off at the drop of a hat, even for things like today." She smiled, hoping to take any sting out of her words. He'd just called her his girlfriend. "I like it a lot. And I could get used to it, easy. But for right now, every time it happens, it's still a very pleasant surprise."

He sat and stared at her for long moments, his expression unreadable. Long enough she lost her nerve and dropped her eyes, tracing mindless figures on her jeans. Jaime finally whispered her fear, "Did I piss you off?"

"No," he answered her gently. "I'm just wondering how I got so lucky to be sitting here. You're not something to solve, not a puzzle. Except for figuring out how I can manage to spend more time with you and Nate." Jaime lifted her gaze, staring at his face, watching as his expression softened. "Jaime, I can pretend to go slower, but my insides are outstripping my outsides right now. I don't have to think...I know. *I love you.*"

Her heart stuttered in her chest, a zing of lightning making her fingers tingle. *He loves me.* She'd been waiting for him to say the words, waiting for him to be certain. As certain as she was. "I love you, too."

He set his plate on the table next to the couch and turned back to her, arms out. "Come here."

Heart in her throat, she went there.

Connor

Ass to Jaime's couch, Connor stretched out one leg, then the other, putting his heels on the coffee table. She was asleep on his lap again, this time facing the back of the couch, her shoulders and one arm draped over his thighs. She stirred and murmured as he moved, and he cupped the back of her neck with one hand, stroking slowly up and down, soothing her back to sleep.

Nate was sitting on the floor at the opposite end of the couch, eyes fixed on the TV where a decades-old movie about superheroes was playing. Jaime had helped quiz him on his homework tonight, while Connor sat at the table with them, nursing a cup of coffee. They'd been quiet for a while, both of them aware she was exhausted and tired, letting her sleep. Nate climbed to his feet, cutting a quick glance at Connor as he scooped his mom's cell phone off the table.

"I'll be back out in a minute, Coach," he muttered, and headed into his bedroom, closing the door softly.

That didn't seem like the kid, he wasn't furtive, and hadn't struck Connor as being the kind to sneak around. After a minute he heard murmuring. Thirsty as well as curious, Connor adjusted Jaime, putting a pillow underneath her head. He walked to the kitchen and filled a glass from the faucet, standing and drinking half of it in one go. Where he stood was significantly closer to Nate's door, and Connor was surprised when he heard Nate raise his voice, the tone firm and angry. "This Marie and Cooper, are they worth this? You think they are, Uncle Jake?" A pause, then, still angry Nate hissed, "*This*."

Another pause and then Nate made a noise, strangled and anguished. "I know you can't know if she won't talk to you. But she's always tired now. And she's too tired to work, which is stressing her out. Most nights she sits at the kitchen table going over the want ads, writing out a list of places to call the next day. She's excited about helping these people, but it's hurting her, Uncle Jake. I hate that." Another pause, indicating Jacob was talking.

Connor warred within himself, trying to decide what to do. As with his students, he wanted to get an idea of the context of the statement before he committed himself to a path. With Jaime suffering from the effects of the medications she'd been taking, it wasn't a leap to understand how Nate could be resentful of the people he saw as the reason for everything.

"*Yes*, I see her looking at want ads." Connor bit back a curse. If Jaime did that in front of Nate, Connor would be surprised. He would expect her to try and hide any anxiety from her son, just as she tried to hide it from him. "She won't tell me she's stressed out, no. Of course not, you know Mom."

"This apartment is twice as expensive as the last one, Uncle Jake." The door creaked again, as if Nate had moved to match the frustration in his voice. "And the last time we were supposed to go to the food bank, she had to go to the clinic. Then she was sick. Again. I'm not telling her, but I'm out of money on my lunch ticket. If she knew, she'd want to make my lunch so I didn't have to eat the free kids' PBJs. We all have to sit at this one table, so we can't get in line for the ticketed kids' food. But we don't have anything to make a lunch out of in the apartment, and worrying about it would stress her out even more."

As he was speaking, Connor's chin slowly dropped until he was staring at the floor. He hadn't known things were that tight for Jaime and her son.

"There was this workbook I needed for labs, but I talked to the teacher, he said I could use one a kid left last semester. So I got that covered, but it's all marked up, and the kid got nearly everything wrong. I'm not telling her about that, either." Nate's voice was louder, and Connor wondered if he should move away from the door. "If I drop out of the high school classes, she wouldn't have to worry about lab fees and things like that." Connor swallowed hard, listening to the kid trying to work through things that would be difficult for an adult. "She was stressed before, but we were okay. Now? Uncle Jake, she's *not* okay."

Another pause, this one shorter, then Nate burst out with, "*No!* You know she won't take money from you. And I'm not asking you for money. That's not why I called." Now Nate's voice was soft, wounded. "I just...Uncle Jakey, I don't have many people to talk to. I shouldn't have said anything." Connor shook his head, swallowing hard at the pain in Nate's voice. "Forget I said anything, okay?"

Without warning the door opened, and Nate stood in the opening, phone in hand, staring at Connor with a look of dawning horror. The words were nearly soundless when he gasped out the question, "You were listening to me?"

Connor held up the half-full glass of water. "Came over for a drink. But you weren't quiet, Nate."

"You weren't supposed to hear." Nate shook his head, looking down, anger and fear warring on his features. "I'm not asking you for money."

"I know you aren't asking for anything, Nate." Jaime stirred on the couch, and Connor walked across and quickly reclaimed his place on the couch, shifting her head back to rest on his leg, stroking her cheek with the backs of his fingers, and waiting for her to slowly settle.

When she did, he looked up, finding Nate still staring at him. "You asked if they were worth it, Coop and Marie. I'm biased because he's my big brother, but I think they are. I've never met a man with a bigger heart. A man who wants to make things better for everyone he meets. When our brother, Cole, died, Coop's the one who kept me on track. If it weren't for him, I don't know where I'd be, honestly. He just kept reminding me, sometimes painfully—" Connor grinned, because he remembered the thumps on the back of his head. "—that I needed to keep putting one foot in front of the other. That there would be something better around the bend. That our parents needed me, that he needed me. That I would one day find a woman—" He looked down at Jaime, fingertips trailing across her cheek, then through her hair to the back of her head. "—and make a family." He looked at Nate, who was staring at him with a guarded expression, one he'd seen before on Jaime's face, the one that said hope was fragile and fleeting, not to be trusted. *I want to change how he feels.*

"That I'd find not just a reason to keep putting one foot in front of the other, but a reason to run. To fly. Cole was my brother, my twin, and we had a special bond. A connection I've never felt with anyone else, before your mother, at least. Coop's the reason I'm sitting here with you. And Marie? She's a woman made to be a mother. Loves her boy Sam, loves him so much it'll tear your heart out to watch her with him. Made to be a mother, but doesn't have that chance on her own. Like I said, I'm biased, but I think that's worth it. Think they're worth it."

"If something happens to Mom, I don't have anyone else." Nate's face turned red as he said this, and he swallowed again, convulsively, clearly fighting back tears. "Uncle Jacob, of course, but he's got Uncle Trent. I researched this, Coach. I know everything bad that can happen."

"It's not going to happen to her, buddy." Connor shook his head. "Not happening." He reached out a hand and waited, relieved when Nate put his palm in Connor's grip. "And you're not alone, Nate. I don't just love your mother." He squeezed the boy's fingers, watching as Nate's eyes took on a sheen of tears. "I love you, too."

"Now, you and me are going to figure out how to make life easier for your mom. You down with that idea?" Nate nodded and Connor grinned.

Standing in his office early the next morning, Connor had to wait through three rings of the phone before it was answered with a brusque, "Cafeteria." Five minutes later he wasn't any closer to sorting out a solution for Nate's lunch ticket.

Nate attended the county school district, while Connor worked in a municipal district further to the east. Frustrated with the runaround he had received from the worker, he finally asked for her supervisor. A short time later he had all the answers he wanted, and information he didn't know what to do with. To his question of, "If I come in with a check, will you apply that to his balance?" the answer has been a resounding "Yes." While that was good news, the bit of disturbing information came when the cafeteria manager mentioned to him that there were a dozen other kids without funds for a hot lunch.

He didn't know what to do with that. The idea that there were kids who fell into a no-man's land between poor enough to receive free lunches, and well enough off to not need assistance didn't sit well with him. Food was such a basic need, and kids were far more vulnerable to the damaging effects of hunger than adults were.

He got his assistant to cover his morning practice, and then drove across town to Nate's campus. On his way to the cafeteria, he stopped at Miles' office, pausing in the open doorway to see his friend bent over the desk, nose nearly touching the notepad he was scribbling on. Glancing up, a quick grin spread over Miles' face, and he pushed to his feet, hand out for a shake. "Thompson," he said, "good to see you. What brings you downtown?"

"Hey, Miles." A quick grip and release, and Connor leaned one shoulder against the doorframe. "Had some business here. Thought I'd stop in and say hey. While I've got you, I have a question for you."

"Shoot." Miles reclaimed his seat, leaning back in the office chair and looking up at Connor.

"You know the gal I'm dating, Jaime Grimes?" Miles nodded. "Her boy goes to school here. Nate—"

Miles interrupted him, a surprised expression on his face. "Nathan Grimes, our wonder boy. Yeah, I know him. Good kid. Smart as a whip, he's confounding everybody. It's been fun to watch him at basketball. Kid's a natural at that, too. His mom's your new squeeze, huh? She must be something special to have wrangled the career bachelor into admitting there's a relationship."

Connor tipped his chin down, studying the floor beyond the toes of his shoes. He'd dated over the years, but never settled into anything serious, and Miles was closer to the mark than Connor found comfortable. "Yeah," he admitted quietly, "she's something else." He glanced up to find Miles looking at him, puzzled. Connor smiled, because being with her, talking about her like this, felt right. "She's amazing. And Nate? He's wonderful right alongside her." Shaking his head, he said, "As nice a topic as my girlfriend is, that's not why I'm here. Do you know if the teachers ever do a fundraiser for the kids? Like the ones who need financial assistance? I came over to drop some cash on Nate's lunch ticket, and found out there's about a dozen kids who are eating PBJs for lunch because they're out of credit. I was thinking of bringing all of their tickets back to current; maybe paying ahead a little bit."

Miles' hand immediately went to his wallet, and he pulled out several bills and extended the money to Connor. "Here, I've paid some of them off before. We've got a challenging economic population here. A lot of the kids are on federal assistance, in housing, or should be. Another whole segment live with family, but not their mom or dad. I'll talk to the office, see if they can let me know when kids are in trouble. We've got a backpack food program, but that only helps on the weekends. Some of these kids, their school meals are all they get during the week, and if that well runs dry, they can be up a creek." Connor leaned over, plucking the money from his grip. "You probably see less of that where you are." He shrugged. "Nothing against this district, it's just a fact of life for our kids. I'm glad Nate has someone like you at his back."

Returning to his campus, Connor walked through the hallways with a more observant eye. In contrast to where Nate was attending, this building had fresh paint and new flooring, even the demeanor of the kids was different. One of the reasons he had pushed to expand the neighborhood basketball program that Nate was in had been to provide positive resources to kids who went to that school.

He had already stalked past the door to the library when he slowed and backtracked, peering in the opening to see one of his players hunched over a table. Fists to either side of his head, Jordan was scowling down at the textbook in front of him. "Jordie, what's up?"

"Coach." The kid offered him a tight smile. "Just cramming. I was trying to keep ahead of the schedule but…" Jordan's voice trailed off, then he sat straight and smoothed his hair back, placing both hands on the table. "Nothing, Coach. I'm good."

Connor coughed a word into his fist, not trying to mask his disbelief, "Liar."

Jordan's smile now was more natural, but still tense and anxious. "No, really, Coach. I'm good. It's just tougher than I expected."

Connor reached out and flipped the book over, keeping Jordan's place with one finger. Shocked, he realized it was one of the books Nate had been working out of last night. An idea started bubbling in his head, and before he could reconsider, he asked Jordan, "You ever consider a tutor?"

"Not really." Jordan shook his head. "I'll get it, Coach. No need for anyone to go out of their way."

That was teenaged boy speak for, "I don't want any of my friends to know I'm struggling." An idea edged its way into Connor's mind, and the more he turned it over, the better it sounded. "How about a trade, then?" Connor knew this would work, it had to. It felt too right not to. "You come help on Saturdays with the basketball clinic and I'll hook you up with someone not at this school who can tutor you for an hour or two."

"Coach." Jordan's eyes dropped to the book and he reached out to slide it closer to him. "I don't really have any cash to pay for tutoring."

"No cash. This is a trade deal. You help me with the kids, and I get my girlfriend's son to tutor you."

"Yeah?" The look on Jordan's face was hopeful and Connor was glad he'd been walking past the library when he had. "That's...that'd be awesome, Coach."

"One thing you need to know about Nate."

"Yeah? What's that?" Jordan slid the book into his bag and shoved his chair back from the table. A quick glance at his watch showed Connor that it was nearly time for the bell to ring.

"He's nine."

Chapter Thirteen

Jaime

"Good job!" Standing on the gym floor next to the stands, Jaime clapped loudly, her palms stinging. She watched Nate advancing up the court slowly, dribbling the ball with practiced control, eyeing the opposing team. Her head jerked and she grinned when he looked one direction, then threw the ball the other, landing it directly into the hands of a teammate who was within range of the hoop. "Yeah, baby. Do it again!" Jittering from foot to foot, she was waiting for a break in the play to run to the bathroom off the hallway.

Whistles blew and she whirled, weaving through the other parents who had chosen to stand rather than be sandwiched between a hundred other people in the stands. Play had already started again when she made her way back to the gym, and she saw Nate was on the bench for this period. There were so many kids his age, they were swapping them in and out in an attempt to give each child equal time on the court.

The anxious look on his face surprised her, and he wasn't even watching the game, he was scanning the stands. *He's looking for me*, she thought, and frowned when his face lit up, knowing that signaled him finding her in the crowd. Hand lifted to her waist, she discretely waved, and then realized she needn't have worried about embarrassing him, because Nate lifted both hands and waved at her, nearly clocking the kid next to him in the head with an elbow. Grinning, she dipped her chin and shook her head.

"Kids sure are something, aren't they?" A man's voice came from the area of her elbow, and she turned her head to see a tall, good-looking man standing nearby. "Give him another year or two and he won't be caught dead waving at his beautiful mother."

Slick, she thought, and fought against rolling her eyes. He'd established he knew kids, implying he had them, and then also worked into the mix that he thought she was attractive. "Kids are something," she agreed, and looked back to the court, trying to discourage without being rude.

"My Johnny's on the bench, too." He wasn't going away. "It doesn't mean they can't play. Johnny's good. He should be out there now. He'd get it done, be all up in the face of that defense."

Confident he couldn't see her face, Jaime allowed the eye roll she'd wanted to do earlier. *Tell the little lady*

161

all about the game, mister. Instead of saying that, she pulled up all the conversations she'd heard between Connor and Nate over the past few weeks. "Of course it doesn't mean they can't play. At this age it's not about being aggressive, or who's best, or even who has aptitude for specific positions, like forward and guard. The idea is to build a love of the game in the kids, and to do that the kids have to be able to explore and find out what fits them best. Understanding teamwork is the byproduct of that. By fourteen, most kids will settle into place, or drop out if b-ball isn't their thing." She shrugged and flicked a glance in his direction to see him staring openmouthed at her. "But they'll take the understanding of teamwork with them throughout their entire life."

He was silent a moment, then in a tone of voice threaded with so much sarcasm she could have scraped it off the walls, he asked, "Coach your hubby?" He made a noise. "Can't be, or he'd be playing his own kid more and not leaving him warming the bench." Another noise, this one disbelieving. "You're just a Monday-morning quarterback."

Connor blew the whistle, signaling time to change players again. "Mixing your sports metaphors?" She giggled, then without looking at him said, "Coach is my boyfriend. And he won't play Nate just to get on my good side."

Silence, and then a sense of absence she confirmed by casting one final sidelong look.

"Baby," Connor murmured against her lips, and she shivered when his tongue dipped into her mouth again. "God, so good."

They were stretched out on her bed, and he had pinned her, one hip on her belly, a thick thigh wedged between her legs. One arm was underneath her shoulders, and the other an iron band angled across her stomach, his hand skating up and down her ribs. She eagerly anticipated every touch, because on the upstroke, his thumb would stroke the underside of her breast, tracing over her shirt, making her breath catch in her throat. On the downstroke, his fingers would spread and cover half her asscheek, clenching and pulling her up against him.

She could feel the heat from his cock, rigid behind his jeans as he rocked against her, her breaths coming faster at the unmistakable evidence that he wanted her. Jaime's hands were splayed on his back, and she trailed one palm up to cup the back of his neck, pulling his mouth back down to meet hers in a kiss that branded her. "Mmhmm." She was so turned on she couldn't even articulate a word, lifting her hips in response to another clutching grip of her ass.

Connor angled his head, teasing her mouth, dragging his tongue across her bottom lip, then following that with a series of playful nips. Easing sideways, he edged down into the bed beside her, resting his head on the pillow so they were face-to-face. The muscles in his jaw were tight, and his voice rasped when he said, "Baby. Killin' me."

Her breathing was as ragged as his, and she found herself arching up against nothing. "Connor," she whispered, watching as he blinked slowly, eyes hooded with arousal. She reached and found his hand, wrapping her fingers around his as she brought it to her waist, impatiently shoving her shirt out of the way and settling his palm on her flesh. Changing grips, she tugged, sliding his hand up her side to her breast. Still not the skin against skin she needed, but the fluttering touch as his fingertips teased along the edge of her bra made her moan. "Please."

"Baby." His hand engulfed her breast, hot, gripping tightly. Her neck twisted at the sudden contact, pressing her head into the pillow. "God," he groaned, "so fuckin' beautiful." Then his mouth was on hers again, the kiss turning desperate and rough, tongues stroking and teeth nipping, biting and tugging on each other's lips. The arm that had been wrapped around her shoulders moved, his hand winding up the back of her neck and into her hair, fingers tangled in her tresses, a grip she didn't want to escape.

Her skin felt on fire, as if her clothes would incinerate any moment and she wished they would, wanted to be skin-to-skin with him, wanted to be under him. "Please." Jaime wasn't even certain her plea hit the air; he ate it down, growling when she pressed up against him, arching into his hand. Then she lost his mouth, lost his hand, felt chilled air as he tugged her shirt up and over her head, fingers working in the middle of her back to loosen and unfasten her bra and that was gone, too. His mouth was on hers again, then he kissed along her jaw, down her neck, pausing to make certain he covered every inch, the satin caress of his lips a thrill. The hand that was back in her hair fisted, turning her head and he kissed her again as he pressed his palm to her breast, catching the hard nipple between two fingers and pinching sharply as he plumped and caressed her and she cried out, needing more.

Mouth to her neck again, he angled her head until he had the access he wanted, laying wet kisses down the column of her throat to her shoulder, biting firmly into the soft muscle in the curve where they joined. *I want him*. His hand on her breast didn't stop its assault, didn't slow and she was moaning deep in her throat, a noise she'd never heard herself make.

He moved, shifted, angling his body so he could continue his exploration, mouth and lips and teeth making themselves known on her chest, then her breast was engulfed in a tight heat that pulled, drawn deep in his mouth as he suckled on her, tip of his tongue flicking across her nipple, pressing it against the roof of his mouth and the sounds she made were louder, harsher. *God!*

Pressure between her legs was perfectly placed, rubbing and gripping, holding tight while he sucked deep again. Her climax was inescapable, building fast, coiling tightly in her belly, tingles shooting down her thighs to the soles of her feet, curling her toes. Then it was on her and it felt like she was levitating, lifted out of her body, cocooned in the ether, then slammed back inside herself, the weight of his body anchoring her while she shivered and shook and he cradled her into his side, wrapping himself around her.

He rocked against her, movements slow and languorous, his hips seeming to move involuntarily as he kissed her mouth softly. Pressing close a final time and dipping between her lips with his tongue, this was a lazy stroke, too. "Jesus, Jaime." He repeated his words from a few moments ago, "So fuckin' beautiful."

She was drifting, curled into him, head on his shoulder, luxuriating in his continued touching of her, his hand slowly stroking up and down her bare back and side when the guilt hit her as she realized he'd gotten her off in spectacular fashion, but hadn't even taken off his own shirt. She flattened her palm on his chest, fabric trapped underneath. "I'm sorry."

Connor froze, then cautiously asked, "For what, honey?"

"I didn't...you didn't." She fisted his shirt and shook it. "I didn't reciprocate." His rich chuckle took her by surprise, and she angled her head to look up into his face, seeing a lazy smile there. "What?"

"You think this is going to be a tit for tat kind of thing? Way off base, baby. I got myself quite the show just now, and you can be assured I enjoyed every single fuckin' second of it. I got to map out some things you like—" He chuckled again. "—some of them much more than others, I'm betting." His arms tightened around her, and she sucked in a quick breath when the fingertips of one hand grazed across her bare breast.

He rumbled, "*Fuck*," then ordered her, "Kiss me." Lifting her chin, she did, giving herself over to the feeling of his lips on hers, working side to side, panting openmouthed against his neck when he moved to kiss her cheek.

Lips to her ear, he whispered, "I also got off, baby. Came so hard in my shorts I'm surprised I didn't blow the fabric to pieces. You're fuckin' hot all the time, but get you in bed and get my hands on you? Unbelievably beautiful and sexy." He kissed her ear, nipping at her earlobe, then whispered, "How's that make you feel, baby? So sexy and gorgeous you got me hot enough to come without using your hands or mouth. Tells me that when we go there, when we can be together like that in just a couple of weeks, when I can be deep inside you as you go off like a rocket, it's going to be phenomenal." Another kiss to the side of her head, and he tightened his arms, squeezing her against his chest. "So much to look forward to." He squeezed her again. "Sleep."

Seated on the bench at the bus stop, she pulled out her phone and texted Connor. The clinic would have already contacted Marie, and Jaime wanted Connor to hear it from her first.

Test was positive. I'm pregnant!

Today was the first time she'd listened to the instructions about intimacy closely. Last night had been amazing, and she'd slept better than in weeks. Connor had stayed the night, the first time he'd done so in her bed, and Nate hadn't even blinked this morning when he'd come out of his room to find Connor already in the kitchen. The clinic required another week of abstinence, but the nurse noted that as she hadn't had a partner when the process began, anyone she had sex with following that period would need to be tested. Nervously Jaime had asked if sperm donors were tested and with a knowing smile the nurse nodded.

She was standing, preparing to board the bus, just waiting on the exiting passengers to clear the way when her phone buzzed in her pocket. Pulling it out once she was seated, she saw a text from Connor. **Wonderful**. A few seconds later a second text arrived. **Celebrate tonight, what sounds good?**

I'll cook, you crazy man. She shook her head as she pressed Send.

In two weeks they'd see the heartbeat on a sonogram. She wasn't even aware she was smiling until the woman beside her said, "That's a happy face. Must have gotten good news."

Turning she saw an older woman, purse in her lap gripped with both hands, smiling broadly at her. "I did. Are you having a good day?"

The woman nodded, then said, "Passable fair. God is good."

"Yes, he is." The bus lurched sideways, and Jaime looked up to see they were approaching the stop at the library. "Hope your day stays good."

"Same to you, sweet child."

As Jaime stepped off the bus her phone buzzed again. Pulling it out, she saw this one was a smiley face from Marie, but she'd missed a text from Connor. His said, ***Call me baby.***

Pressing the phone icon from his contact info, she waited for him to answer, then immediately said, "Baby."

Silence for a moment, then Connor asked, "What, honey?"

"You told me to call you baby, so I did."

"Do you always do what you're told, Miss Grimes?" His voice dipped low, teasing, and she smiled as she walked into the library, waving at the volunteer at the desk. "If so, I can tell you that is one thing I will plan entire nights around exploiting."

"Goofy man." *I can't remember when I've smiled as much*, she thought, pulling a chair out from under one of the tables in the computer lab. "Why did you want me to call, Connor?"

"I need a list."

"A list for what?" She sat and leaned forwards, elbow to the table, chin in her hand as she talked on the phone, speaking quietly out of respect for the library's patrons.

169

"Groceries." He chuckled. "If I don't have a list, it's a dangerous proposition for me to hit the store. I have terrible impulse control when it comes to spices and condiments."

As he spoke, Jaime felt her smile fading. Money again. "I can buy groceries, Connor."

"But you're cooking." She waited, but he didn't continue.

"If that's your whole argument, you might as well hang up, because you already lost. Most men would probably offer to clear the table in exchange for a cooked meal." Jaime let her eyes sink closed, shutting out the sight of the books and people wandering the shelves. "Plus, I don't cook fancy. I have all the spices and condiments I need."

"I have to go to the store anyway, pick up snacks for Saturday and Sunday." His high school team had a tournament this weekend, and would be gone from Saturday morning until late Sunday. "If you go to the store, you have to lug stuff home on the bus. I have a truck. So many reasonable arguments, Jaime. Send me a list, honey."

"You don't need to do that."

"Send me a list."

"Connor." Her tone was sharper than she'd intended, but he was frustrating her.

Tolerant but determined, he repeated, "Jaime, send me a list." He hesitated, then said softly, "Please, baby?"

"You're impossible, you know that, right?" Tipping her head to the side, she rested her cheek in her upturned palm. "What time will you be at the apartment?"

"I'll be home about six. Short practice tonight, all the kids have tests tomorrow."

Jaime nearly couldn't choke out any words. He'd called her apartment home. "Okay."

"Are you all right?" His question came immediately, telling her she hadn't been able to keep her emotions from her voice.

"I'm fine." She cleared her throat, trying to get rid of the gravelly tone. "Hormones."

His voice was warm when he responded, "Okay. I'll see you at six." He paused, then reminded her, "List, baby."

"Okay."

"Right there." The tech leaned over as she turned the sonogram machine around and pointed at the screen. "See the fluttering? That's the heartbeat. You made a baby!"

Jaime craned her neck, looking up to see Marie and Cooper embracing, staring at the screen. Fingers squeezed her hand and she turned to look into Connor's eyes. He smiled at her then turned his attention to his brother and sister-in-law. "Congratulations, Mom and Dad," he said, and she smiled.

Sarah stood behind the tech, watching the occupants of the crammed-full room. She gave the Thompsons a moment to celebrate, then brought everyone's attention back to the monitor. "We'll finish up with the sono, make sure we're looking at a single heartbeat. I know everyone's excited, but we need to keep things moving along. Jaime,"—she looked down, one side of her mouth quirking up—"you and I can chat after the procedure, so when you're done in here, come and see me, okay?"

Jaime nodded, saying, "Okay." The tech turned the machine again and got back to work. When they were done, Marie and Cooper left with the good news that they had a single baby, no multiples, and it was well placed. Connor waited in the hallway for Jaime as she walked to Sarah's office and knocked.

At the welcoming call of "Come in," Jaime pushed the door open and saw Sarah seated behind her desk. "Quite a journey, huh?"

Settling into the chair across from Sarah, Jaime nodded, saying, "Yes, it really is. I'm so happy for the Thompsons. This is amazing."

"It really is. This part never gets old, getting to see the faces of the parents as they realize all the hard work and money has been worth it." Jaime pulled a paper from a folder and slid it across to Jaime. "Speaking of money, here's the check documentation. Like last time, I just need you to sign it and then I'll authorize the transfer to your account."

Jaime took the pen Sarah passed her, scribbling her name on the recipient line without looking at the paper too closely. "Thank you, Sarah." She stood when Sarah did and leaned across the desk to shake her hand and gave her a folded piece of paper.

"You're very welcome, Jaime. Here's your copy of the paperwork. We'll see you in a couple of weeks, make sure the girls set-up the appointment before you leave."

Turning in the doorway, Jaime nodded and waved, then pulled the door shut behind her. Connor rose from the chair he'd been occupying, and reached for her hand just as Jaime opened the folded paper. It was twice the amount she'd been expecting, and her heart stuttered in her chest. Ignoring Connor, she whirled and knocked on Sarah's door, opening it immediately. "Sarah, there's a mistake."

Sarah laughed and leaned forwards to rest her elbows on the desk. "I wondered when you'd notice."

"It's too much. This isn't what we agreed to." Combine this with the odd payment at the beginning, and Jaime was feeling very much like a fraud. "It's way too much."

"The agreement you signed lays out the minimum amount of each payment along the way." Sarah shook her head, still smiling. "It doesn't say anything about denying an increase if the contracting couple wants to provide such. This doesn't change any of the other payments, Jaime. It's all very standard, I promise you."

"Standard?" That didn't seem right, but she could understand why Sarah wouldn't want to mention it beforehand, because a surrogate or gestational carrier might come to expect it, and be disappointed if their check were only the contracted amount. "You're sure it's not a mistake?"

"Not a mistake," Sarah shook her head, then made a shooing motion with one hand, smiling broadly. "Go on, get home and put your feet up. You're a certified baby maker now."

Jaime pulled the door shut again, looking up at Connor. She could see the question in his eyes, and for a moment she wondered if he knew what his brother had done. "Ready to go home?" He'd driven them this morning, taking another day off work. *At this rate, he won't have any vacation left*, she thought wryly, hoping his family didn't take group trips.

"Yes," he answered, trailing his fingers down her arm until he clasped her hand. As they walked through the front doors of the clinic, he asked, "What's next for the baby?"

"After the next sono, it's just regular visits at the OB offices near the hospital. No more IVF clinic." She climbed up into the truck and leaned back, his routine of buckling her in now familiar. Connor brushed his lips across hers, and she smiled as he shut the door.

Connor

"You ever gonna tell her?" Cooper's voice was quiet, and since he'd already said Marie and Sam were sleeping, that was to be expected. "You know, what you did?"

"Probably." Connor lifted his beer and took a pull. "Yeah, definitely. After we've been married about five years. That oughta be just enough time to have her forever tied to me."

Cooper laughed softly. "Sarah said she wanted to argue the money. I swear, Jaime would almost be happier if she were just doing this because she and Marie are friends."

"She said as much tonight. Said she feels like a fraud, because she might have started because she needed the money, but she's entirely about the fact that she's helping the two of you now." Connor sighed. "I love her, Coop."

"I know you do, little brother. You tell her yet?"

Connor smiled. "Yeah. Dad said to follow my heart. So I did."

"She leave ya hangin'?"

"Not a bit of it. My girl caught me and gave it right back to me." Connor finished the beer, staring at the TV he'd muted when the phone rang. "We get this surrogate thing done, and I'm asking her to marry me. Won't be giving her months to get ready, either. She pops your kid

175

out and I'm hauling her ass to Vegas. I'll propose in front of Elvis, and he can do the honors before she cottons on to what I'm saying."

Cooper laughed. "I'm glad you got that, bro."

"Me, too, man." Connor smiled. "Me, too."

Chapter Fourteen
Jaime

She stood at the kitchen sink, chin to her chest, looking down at her hand resting on her still-flat belly. *Tonight*, she thought, and smiled. Nate would be heading home with a friend after school to spend the weekend. Connor didn't have any games or practices until Monday. They had two nights together, and she had the doctor's official approval, with the caveat they not do anything too strenuous. Jaime's smile widened into a grin. *Two nights.*

As if on cue, her phone rang and the display said, *Connor calling …*

"Hey there," she said when she answered. "How was school today?"

"Good as it can be with hundreds of insolent future leaders of our nation all planning their takeover coup."

The humor in his tone belied his words, and she laughed. "Don't laugh. I caught three of the senior boys passing a tablet back and forth. They were using mapping software to work through the best and easiest way to drive to Nashville and back without their parents knowing. Seems one of them got invited to a frat party, planning on being the early kid on campus, I guess." Connor chuckled. "Not sure who looked more disappointed the weekend plans were waylaid, the parents or the kids."

"Wow," she breathed, "I'm going to go out on a limb and say the parents. Are you coming over soon?" *Like now?* She smiled at her thoughts.

"I'm on my way, baby. Be there in ten." His voice was soft with a smile, and when he continued speaking, an edge of rough crept in. "You got plans tonight?"

"Every plan I have in my head begins and ends with you." Before Connor, she would never have been so bold, never have put herself out there with a statement like that. Once again, he proved she didn't have anything to worry about, responding in kind.

"God, I love when you say things like that. I can't wait to touch you," his voice sounded like it was filled with gravel, "and taste you."

"Drive safely," she whispered.

"On my way," he confirmed. "See you soon."

"See you soon."

Knowing he was only minutes away sent her into a flurry of activity as she straightened the living room and kitchen, quickly tidying some of Nate's things, and putting away the clean dishes. She took the lid off the slow cooker where she had a whole chicken along with vegetables, testing the doneness of the potatoes and turning down the cooker. That was where she was when she heard Connor's key in the door.

Standing at the kitchen counter, she remembered the first night Connor had come into the apartment using that key. She hadn't given it to him, Nate had, which was the biggest act of implied approval she'd ever heard of. Afterwards, Nate had been cool about it, but let her know in no uncertain terms that he expected Connor would be over a lot. *"We're on the couch and he gets home from school, we could spill the popcorn getting up to let him in,"* Nate told her with a grin. *"This way Coach sets the stage for his own entrance."*

"God." The rasping tone hadn't left his voice during the drive; if anything it was deeper, rougher. Chin over her shoulder, she watched him stalking across the room towards her. He came up behind her, fitting himself to her and wrapping his arms around her waist, tugging her against his front. "I can't believe my luck." Mouth to the side of her neck, he kissed and nibbled the tendon exposed when she arched her neck, offering him better access. "A woman as hot and sexy as you—" The kisses trailed up her neck to her ear, and latching onto her earlobe with his teeth, he tugged before whispering, "all mine."

She didn't know when she'd caught her lip between her teeth, but it took blowing a deep breath out before she could release her hold to answer. "Hi, Connor."

Mouth to her neck again, he murmured, "Hi, Jaime." His arms gave her a squeeze before one of them relaxed, his hand slipping up her side, thumb caressing the underswell of her breast, a slow back and forth that quickly built a fire inside her. "Miss me, honey?"

Nodding, she tipped her head back against his shoulder. His other arm moved south, and his big hand cupped her hip, tugging her tightly against him as he arched into her, his hot erection pushing and straining, cradled between the cheeks of her ass.

"Too fast to move this straight to the bedroom?" He kissed the hinge of her jaw and she lifted her head, meeting his mouth and opening for him. Turning in his arms, she wrapped her hands around the back of his neck, rising up on her toes to offer him more. His palms slid down and cupped her ass, the hard brand of his cock pressing against her belly. A moment later he was walking her backwards towards the bedroom door, mouth never leaving hers.

In the dimly-lit bedroom, he took his time undressing her, fingers and mouth covering every inch of skin he exposed, branding her with his touch. When she was bare before him, he threaded his fingers between hers, pulling her arms around him and placing her hands low against his back as he bent his head, fitting his mouth to hers in a long, deep, wet kiss. A soul-searing kiss, one that seemed to go on forever, but didn't last nearly long enough. His hands came up from where they rested on her waist, skimming up her sides until he cradled her face between his palms. Pulling back, he stared down into her eyes, and she shivered at his expression. Intense, and focused, his eyes were dark with arousal.

"I love you, Jaime."

The moment held and stretched, and, voice stolen by the powerful emotion gripping her, she mouthed the words back at him, "I love you, Connor."

Then his clothes were off, strewn around the room in much the same fashion hers were, and he was laying her back against the mattress, stretching out beside her. Propped up on an elbow, he leaned over and kissed her, closed mouth at first, firm, as if he were impressing himself on her. Then he teased along her bottom lip with his tongue, and she opened, while the kiss blazed up and out of control. Delving into her mouth, he tangled his tongue with hers, stroking and twisting, teeth nipping. His hand landed on the inside of her knee and he curled his fingers around, tugging up and to the side, letting her thigh rest against his hip. Opened like that, she had no defense against his touch, groaning when he slid his hot palm up her thigh to cover her center. With the heel of his hand resting just above her clit, his fingers slipped and slid through her folds, teasing her opening, circling while he applied pressure, all while he deepened the kiss, eating down her moans.

She lifted a hand, cradling the back of his head, fingers exploring there as his were below. She traced the whirls of his ear, felt the silky texture of his hair slipping between her fingers, scratched lightly at his scalp. Nipping at his bottom lip, she pulled a groan out of him and smiled against his mouth when his hips jerked, his hard cock bouncing against her hip where she pressed against him.

She pulled back and he lifted a fraction of an inch, staring into her eyes as his hand continued its gentle torture. Fingers threaded through his hair, she held his gaze, waiting. Lifting her hips, she urged him to do what she knew he wanted, had held back from during their time together. "Please," she said on a breath, pumping up with her hips again. He stilled for a moment, then pressed one thick finger inside her and she heard herself groan, head arching back into the pillow.

Connor

Watching Jaime give herself over to him was the single hottest thing Connor had ever seen. *Jesus*, he thought, slowly driving his middle finger in and out of her scorching channel. She kept her hold on his hair, and the sweet sting of her pull on his scalp pushed him higher, made his dick impossibly harder. He bent his neck and kissed her, groaning when she met him halfway, as hungry for him as he was her.

He'd been ready for her all day, ever since he got her text after the doctor visit this morning. ***Green means go***. Yeah, go wasn't a problem when he was lying in bed next to her, naked, skin-to-skin. Come, now that was a different story. Everything threatened too soon, and this was an event he wanted to savor.

Teasing and circling her opening, he paired ring finger to middle one and slowly pushed both inside her, stretching and preparing her for him. They'd talked often over the past weeks as they kissed and petted, and he knew she hadn't taken a lover for years, her life too busy with keeping hearth and home together for her son. Jaime had laughed hard one night while they were watching TV, some silly sitcom where the ditzy blonde lead was talking about revirginizing being a thing. Face buried against his chest in an effort to quiet her laughter, Jaime had choked out, "I've been revirginized."

Might as well be true, he thought, panting against her mouth at the sensation of her muscles clutching hungrily at his fingers. *Sleek and tight, hot as hell.* "Fuck," he gritted out, pumping in and out of her, "wet and hot, baby." He wanted to make her come, wanted to give her that. "Give you everything, baby."

"Connor." Her whisper ghosted across his lips, and he bent his neck, breaking the kiss to lap at her nipple, pulling it between his lips and teeth, drawing deep. "God," she gasped, her body twisting against his, her hand slipping up and down the back of his neck in time with his fingers plunging into her. She stiffened, still moving, but tense and tight, on the brink. Mouth to her nipple, he grazed the tender flesh with his teeth, pushing his fingers deep and pressing down on her clit with his thumb, circling and gliding back and forth until she moaned again, this a wordless cry while she tightened around him.

He shifted, withdrawing his fingers, pushing her other leg wide so he fell between them, hips lined up with hers as he thrust, clenching his ass to try and hold back. The head of his cock rubbed between her folds, engulfing him in heat and wet, slippery fire on his shaft. Then he tipped his hips, and the crown nudged at her opening. A blazing pressure engulfed him as he slowly pushed inside a couple of inches.

She'd stilled and quieted as she came down from the heights to which he'd driven her, and now as he began his possession of her body, she came back to herself, came back to him. Hips tipping and tilting, she angled to take in more of him, hands slipping and smoothing up his sides and back. "Please," she whispered, lips to his ear. "More, Connor. I need more."

Yes, baby, he thought, and bowed his back, pushing forwards with his hips, leading the way with his cock, pressing deeper into her. "All for you, Jaime." Gasping with the effort of holding back, not wanting to hurt or frighten her, he felt the muscles in his ass and thighs jerking. "Feels so good, baby. Perfect."

"Yes, perfect," she echoed, and he felt the scrape of her nails against his shoulder. "God, Connor, move. Con, *please*."

Then she clenched down on his cock, muscles rippling and milking, pulling him deeper. With a growl, he pushed, seating himself inside her, feeling the heat of her ass on his balls, juices from her pussy soaking his shaft. "You want me to move, baby?" His words had an edge of threat in them, and he knew she read it correctly when she responded immediately with another clutching grip on his cock. "Jesus, Jaime." He pulled out halfway and eased back in, deep, grinding the base of his cock against her clit, feeling the little puffs of her panting breaths against the skin of his neck and shoulder. Sweat-slicked, their bellies slid across each other, and he tipped his head, lifting on his elbows to look down their bodies.

In the low light of the room, he saw her curves, breasts slightly flattened on her chest, nipples drawn tight on their peaks. The barely-there swell of her belly, rounded handles of her hips, and then he pulled out halfway again to see the glistening sheen of her arousal on his cock. "God, look at you." He lifted his gaze to her face, seeing her eyes were focused on him, hooded and filled with lust and love. "So fucking beautiful. Look at us." He pressed inside her again, then shifted, pushing up on his hands so he could see better. "Look at how we fit together." Halfway out, he paused, tightening his stomach muscles, pulling his cock up, twitching it inside her so she gasped his name. "You're perfect, Jaime." Deep inside her, he watched as she took him, seeing the glide of his cock as he seated himself again. "So fucking beautiful."

"So good, Connor." Her mouth opened, lips forming an O as she panted. "Perfect," she agreed, eyes clenching tight as her head thrust back into the pillow.

He dropped down to his elbows, muscles in his arms shaking as he buried his face against her shoulder. "Love you, honey." Ass and back working, flexing and arching, bowing in turn, he plunged in and out, building, chasing, while she met him stroke for stroke, her hips lifting, arms by turns tight around him as she held on, and clasping as she rode the edge of her orgasm. "I'm close," he warned her, wrapping his arms underneath her, holding her tight against him. "Baby."

"So close." She breathed the words out on a huff of air, and he moved, shifting to push one hand down between them, pressing his thumb against her clit. That was what it took for her, and she exploded underneath him, bucking and writhing, trying to get closer and get away at the same time. Her inner muscles tightened around him, clutching him desperately so he had to fight to keep rhythm, and then he was falling over the same wall she'd climbed. He roared as his balls drew tight to his body, electricity shooting down his legs and then back up, detonating at the base of his spine.

Grunting, wordless, he rocked deep, then deeper, feeling his cock pulsing inside her, surrounded by heat and tight flesh as he came. Slowly he came back to himself, feeling the silky strokes of her palms up and down his back. "Jaime," he whispered, his voice choked because of the beauty she'd given him. "You okay?"

"If by okay, you mean more relaxed than I've ever been in my life? Then yes, I'm okay." She nuzzled the side of his head, pressing a kiss to his ear. "Better than okay, silly man. You are as fabulous in bed as you are out of it." Smiling at her words, he lifted and looked down at her.

"You're no slouch yourself, woman. Holy shit, that was hot as hell." Bending his neck, he pecked her lips with a quick kiss. "Lemme get a washcloth. I'll get us cleaned up." Leaning in closer, he kissed her again, more slowly, possessing her mouth with his. "Amazing, baby." Putting his mouth to her ear, he whispered softly, hoping to set any final fears to rest. "So very worth the wait."

Chapter Fifteen
Jaime

Standing up from the couch where she and Nate had been caught up in a Sunday afternoon monster movie marathon, Jaime lifted her arms and stretched. As she arched her back, she felt the fluttering in her belly again. Stronger this time than it had been in the past few weeks, she cradled her belly with one palm and experienced the sensation against her hand for the first time as the baby rolled and tumbled inside her.

Life was an amazing thing. She smiled down at Nate where he was sprawled on the floor in front of the couch, eyes still on the TV. Scattered around him was the detritus of his snacking, and she bent over to start gathering up the empty bowls he'd used for chips, cookies, and popcorn.

The days are just flying past, she thought, straightening up, a little out of breath. *Five months*. Her next regular visit to the OB would be tomorrow. *Hard to believe*. Walking to the kitchen sink with the dishes in her hands, she glanced over her shoulder at Nate as he asked, "When's Coach coming over?" She smiled at his unstated acceptance of how Connor had fit himself into their lives.

"Not tonight," she told him. "He's getting ready for the state tests. Seems even the history teacher has work to do this time of year." At least basketball was over for a couple of weeks. The last four weeks before winter break had been brutal, with much of his time taken up by the team and games. She'd been stuck in the queasy turmoil of morning sickness that really was an all-day sickness for a few weeks, and hadn't gotten to see him as often as either of them would have liked. "He'll be here tomorrow night for dinner."

They'd argued last night, not a fight, just a back and forth differing of opinion about tomorrow's doctor's appointment. He'd gone with her to the first ones, wanting to get a feel for the doctor. She felt guilty when he organized his life around her like that, and with this being a busy week, she'd finally put her foot down. No way did he need to take another day off, or even a morning off to go to a routine appointment, when what he needed was to be in his classroom. Marie and Cooper would be there, of course, excited to hear the rapid and strong heartbeat of the baby.

"What do you want to watch next?" Nate called, not having moved from his reclining position. "More creature features, or want to see this thriller?"

"Both ideas have merit." She laughed as she turned back to him. "I'm thinking...thriller." The look on his face surprised her; he wore an expression of intense fear, eyes opened so wide the whites shone in the lights. "What's wrong?"

"Mom, what's wrong?" he said at the same time, lurching to his feet. "Are you okay?" Shaking her head, she stared at him as he lifted a hand and pointed to her middle. "You're bleeding."

Scanning down, she saw the juncture of her legs was dark, with what looked like blood seeping into the fabric. *Shit*. "Let me go to the bathroom, honey. I'll be right back." Once the door closed behind her, she pulled down her sweatpants and underwear, looking at the blood smeared across her upper thighs. Her heart rate increased until she could hear it in her ears. This wasn't spotting. This was bleeding. Redressing, she exited to find a clearly frightened Nate in the hallway, phone in his hand.

"What do I do, Mom?" Glancing at the phone, she saw he'd pressed 911, and his thumb was hovering over the green button.

"Nothing yet, let me get changed." In her bedroom, she stripped off the stained clothing, digging a pad out of her purse as she pulled on clean clothes. Panic started to set in as she thought, *Twenty weeks, it's too early. I'm just five months*. Taking a steadying breath, she opened the door. Holding her hand out for the phone, she said, "I need to call the doctor." A few minutes later she and Nate were crawling into the backseat of a cab.

At the ER, the aide at the desk took forever to take her information, and Jaime held tight to the knowledge that she hadn't experienced cramping. Not once. In the exam room, she handed the phone and her purse to Nate as he stepped outside to sit in a chair in the hallway. Then the doctor began his evaluation, barking orders at a nurse who was in the room. Jaime lost track of what they were doing, holding one arm out for one woman to draw blood, resting her other arm at her side while a cuff tightened and loosened on her bicep, feeding information to the machine beeping near the wall.

"Doctor?" The white-coated man was reading a paper but lifted his eyes to her at her question. A tech tightened a band around her belly, positioning a monitor along the bottom edge of the swell the baby made in her lower stomach. "Should I call the parents?" She reminded him of something she'd said a dozen times already, "I'm a surrogate."

Just as he said, "Not yet, Miss Grimes," she heard a commotion in the hallway. A gruff, familiar voice asking, "Jaime Grimes. Where is she?" Then Nate yelled, "Coach," and Jaime took her first deep breath in what seemed like forever.

Connor didn't ask permission, he didn't wait for someone to open the curtain for him, he just pushed through and a moment later had his arms tight around

191

her. Jaime clutched at his shoulders, burying her face against his chest as he kissed the side of her head, whispering into her ear, "I'm here, baby. I'm here."

"Mister Grimes?" The doctor tried to regain control of the situation.

Connor corrected him, saying, "Connor Thompson."

That made the doctor look down at the paperwork with a frown. "Says here the parents of the fetus are Thompson."

"My brother and his wife." Connor hadn't released her, hadn't eased his grip, and Jaime was glad. Then she felt him shift, and the familiar smell of Nate teased her nose so she angled her head and looked down to see her son had wiggled his way between them, creating a space for himself in the middle of the hug, and was held in place there by Connor's big hand. "This is my family, Doc. Tell me what's going on."

"Miss Grimes?" Now the doc was looking at her with one lifted brow, asking if he should include Connor in whatever he was about to say. She nodded, and he quirked a grin at her, then said, "Nothing definitive, yet. Miss Grimes experienced some spontaneous bleeding and came to the emergency room on the advice of her OB."

The tech made one final adjustment and stepped back, turning on the machine behind her and the area filled with the rapid, booming sounds of the baby's heartbeat. The tech rattled off some numbers to the doctor who nodded. "Everything so far is looking—" He smiled at Jaime. "—and sounding good. We're going to monitor for a while, make sure nothing is going on that we haven't uncovered yet. The bleeding was unexpected and isn't something we generally see at this point in pregnancy, so I want to be sure we're looking at everything. The good news is it didn't sound like there was much bleeding"—Jaime shook her head, because when she got to the hospital the pad she'd put on hadn't much discharge on it—"and there's no cramping"—she shook her head again—"and we've got a good, strong fetal heartbeat. Wait and see, and while I know those aren't reassuring words, they should be. The fact we aren't scurrying around is a good thing, Miss Grimes."

He turned and stepped out, followed by the nurse and tech, and then it was just her, Connor, and Nate. She took a deep breath, then another, realizing suddenly that her fingers were clutching at Connor's shirt, holding him tight. "I'm so glad you're here, Connor."

Mouth to the top of her head, Connor murmured, "I'm glad Nate called me. Good job, buddy." His arms squeezed. "We'll talk later about why you didn't call sooner, Jaime." Clearing his throat, he asked, "Is that the baby's heartbeat?" Jaime nodded, not lifting her head from his chest. Softly, reverently, he whispered, "So strong."

Nate squirmed out from between them, and Jaime looked up to see a smile flash across his face. "Mom, can I play that farming game on your phone if I get on the hospital Wi-Fi?" She nodded, and he eased through the curtains, and she heard the plastic chair move, signaling he had planted his butt, a sentinel.

"Nate called you, huh?" She'd thought of calling Connor a dozen times, starting from when she first saw the blood, and ending with just before he'd shown up at the hospital. "He was scared."

"I was scared too, baby." Connor's words were soft, and she twisted to look up at him. "He said you were sick, so I told him I'd be right over, then he let me know you weren't home, you were at the ER. I was terrified the whole drive." He pressed his lips together, jaw firm, and then asked, "Why didn't you call me?"

"After I called my doctor and he said to get to the ER, things went fast. Then we were here, and before I had a chance, here you were, too." Closing her eyes, she leaned against him. "Thank you for coming."

"Nowhere else I'd rather be, baby." Brushing his lips against the side of her head, he repeated, "Nowhere else."

The fluttering in her belly woke her, and Jaime's hand dropped to cover the baby bump, feeling the skin stretch and move with the baby. She heard, "No, she's sleeping now, just dozed off. Doc said there's nothing to worry about, nothing wrong with the pregnancy."

Connor was outside in the hallway, leaning against the wall. Seen through a gap in the curtains, he seemed to be looking down at Nate sleeping awkwardly in the chair. In response to a question from the phone, he expanded on his answer, "Jaime's good. She's fine. Doc said she's perfect." A pause, then he confirmed who he was talking to by saying, "Yeah, Coop. She's perfect for me. With my heart in my throat the whole way over, I must have run a dozen red lights. Thank God Nate called me." He shook his head, one hand reaching out to gently tousle Nate's hair. "He had her phone and was scared. Hell, they were both scared." She saw one corner of his mouth quirk up. "I heard the baby's heartbeat. That's some powerful mojo, man. I can't wait to see it born." Another pause, then, voice gruff, he said, "Yeah, get some sleep. I'll call and let you know what's going on in the morning."

She turned to her side, feeling the monitor strapped to her belly poke her awkwardly, the heartbeat changed in volume and Connor looked up and met her eyes through the space in the curtains she'd been using to watch him. He moved, stepping inside, and softly said, "Hey, you're supposed to be sleeping."

Jaime smiled up at him, and he leaned over, brushing her mouth with his. "The little acrobat woke me."

"Baby's moving? That's good, right?" Connor slipped his palm up and down her arm, slowly, soothingly.

Another jolting flutter and Jaime grinned. "Wanna see if you can feel him?"

"Him?" One corner of Connor's mouth lifted, and he crinkled his nose. "You think it's a boy?"

"I don't know what it is, but I can't call it 'it.' That feels weird." Jaime slipped to lie flat on her back, reaching up to capture Connor's hand. She brought it to her belly, and pressed firmly, holding his palm in place. "Wait for it." Another strong flutter and Jaime saw Connor's face light up, a broad smile settling into place. "Feel that?" He nodded.

"That's crazy." His whisper was quiet and filled with awe.

She shook her head, seeing him register another movement of the baby inside her. "That's life."

Connor

Hands on the grips of the wheelchair, he watched as Jaime listened carefully to the nurse, accepting the sheet of discharge instructions in one hand, the other wrapped around Nate's waist, holding her son close. It felt as if they were lightyears away from the sterile examination room where his life had changed. For the past hour he'd gone over each of those moments a thousand times, picking apart the emotions that had flooded him when he'd heard the heartbeat, so loud and strong, and then felt the baby move inside her.

Beautiful and terrifying in the same breath.

I love her so much.

Nate twisted, looking up at Connor with a grin and he returned it, tightening his grip on the handles. *Love him, too*. He'd known Jaime less than a year, but couldn't imagine being without her. He hadn't been kidding when he talked to Cooper a few hours ago, Connor had never known fear like earlier, when Nate called him. *Mom's bleeding, Coach. We're at the hospital*. He scarcely remembered the drive, everything a blur except the few drivers fool enough to get in his way, moved by his horn and screaming face, shaking fists.

She's okay, he reminded himself, shutting down the following thought of what if she hadn't been, because that didn't factor. She was okay.

The concerned expression on the nurse's face caught his attention, and he zoned back in on what they were saying. "Miss Grimes, it's best if you have someone with you for a couple of days. Are you sure there's no one you can call?'

Connor interjected, "I'll be with her." Jaime twisted in the chair, looking up at him and releasing her hold on Nate, who stepped away with a grin on his face. Connor gave her a pretend scowl. "Don't even start, baby. You need me? I'm there. Should know by now there's no getting rid of me."

Gazes locked for a moment, then two, and she slowly shook her head. "Hyperdrive." She reminded him of his own word, and he bent to press his lips to her forehead. "Okay." She gave in and he kissed her again. She gasped and he pulled back when she whispered, "Acrobat."

197

He couldn't help himself, wanting to cement the memory of what they'd shared earlier, he reached and put one palm against the swell of her belly to feel the movement inside her again. The same sense of loss swept over him, he was ecstatic and incredibly sad at the same moment. Overwhelmed, and guilty at the persistent thought that circled around and around in his head.

I put it there, but it's not mine.

Chapter Sixteen
Jaime

"God, I want you," he growled, mouth to her ear as he swept up her back with his palm. He fitted himself against her, his erection nestled against her ass. Jaime stretched and sighed, rolling her head to offer her mouth. Connor had been away at a game tonight, one she'd listened to on the radio, picturing him as the announcer talked about him stalking up and down the sidelines, shouting encouragement to his kids, arguing with the referees. Nate had stayed home with her, fingers flying over his scientific calculator as he worked out the problems assigned as part of his homework.

Now Connor was home, and naked, and in their bed. Jaime moaned when he possessed her mouth, tongues tangling hotly. When he pulled back for a breath, she responded to his demand. "Then have me, Connor."

199

The day following her whirlwind ER visit, she had gotten the all clear from her OB. No explanation for the bleeding, but no expectation that it would repeat. Under orders to take it easy for a few days, Connor had taken that to extremes, keeping her in his apartment and ensuring she didn't lift anything heavier than a glass of water. A week later, the first time she had initiated sex he had nearly freaked out afterwards, hovering and so worried she couldn't laugh.

He had coaxed her into abandoning her job search for now, too, arguing that she had the resources to take a breather from what had to be a stressful activity. She'd nervously agreed, and had to admit he was right. It gave her more time with Nate, and with Connor, too. Something they both enjoyed.

She'd come to understand she was precious to him. To believe.

She rolled to her back and he adjusted, propping himself up on one arm so he could lean across her for a kiss. Slanting his mouth on hers, she felt his fingers start at her knee and skim her nightgown up her side, heat from his touch branding the path he laid on her skin. Jaime bent her outside leg, angling it wide, inviting his touch there, too. He accepted the invitation, fingertips tracing along the edge of her underwear. She lifted her hips, and his fingers slipped under the fabric as her breath caught in her throat, held there by the sensation of him touching her.

"God, Jaim," he gritted the words out, rocking against her hip. "So hot and wet, God." His fingers curled around the side of her panties, tugging and pulling, stripping them down her legs. Back to her core, he palmed her roughly, applying pressure to her clit and the flesh around it, knowing what she liked. One finger inside, then two, and he plunged them in time with his tongue's assault on her mouth, pulling her higher and higher. She pumped up against him, and he groaned. "Yeah, fuck yourself on my fingers. So fucking hot." Teeth to her bottom lip, he bit and tugged, sucking it into his mouth as his fingers thrust deep while she came, clenching around him.

He moved, tugging her inside leg high over his hip and he fit himself to her in that position, rocking into her while on his side. She dug her heel into his ass, lifting and moving with him, and he groaned again, rasping her name out as he slipped deeper. "Jaime, fuck." His thigh moved forwards and she rolled slightly.

"Connor." All she could say was his name, and it became a chant as she felt the tightness swelling inside her again. "Con, honey." His hand curved over her hip, fingers to her clit as he worked back and forth. "Connor."

"I love you." She turned her head, watching his face as he repeated his words. "I love you, Jaime." Mouth open, he sucked in a harsh breath and then stilled, muscles quivering. "God."

"I love you, Connor." She got that much out before her orgasm swept over her, pulling her eyes closed. "Love you."

Chapter Seventeen
Jaime

"There's almost four months left on the lease, Connor. I can't just up and move." This had become a frequent refrain in the past three months. "What if I told them I'm not going to renew, should I go ahead and do that?" She walked up the stairs to his apartment, grocery bag in one hand, purse on her shoulder.

His rumbling approval sounded through the phone, and she grinned at his words, "Not like you spend a lot of time there. I want you and Nate moved into my place soon, honey. Settle us. Even if you leave it empty and pay the rent, I want you in my place." He paused, then his voice dropped an octave, "Our place."

"If I move, maybe if they lease it, they'll release me?" She hadn't considered moving out while still paying rent, an idea which went against every frugal bone in her body, but Connor was right, the few nights they spent at her and Nate's apartment were for convenience, mostly. Her place was closer to the doctor's office, so they would usually all stay there the night before an appointment, and head back to Connor's apartment the other nights. The only challenge was getting Nate to school, but that was a chore Connor seemed happy to take care of, driving her son to the downtown school every morning.

"They might, honey. If they lease it, I bet they'd have to. The manager's not a dick, so I bet he'll understand."

There was sound in the background, and she laughed, asking, "Is that a duck?"

"Yeah, Mom got some Indian Runners for the pond. They're in a box in the backseat of the truck right now." He sighed. "Dabblers are supposed to be good for the dam. Daddy just rolls his eyes at her and writes the check. Nate and I'll put 'em in the barn for the night, then take them to the pond in the morning."

"When are my boys coming home?" Connor had been at his parents' for most of the past week, helping with the more strenuous chores surrounding the planting season. Cooper had asked him to go, citing memories of past springs. With school on a break, the two men had taken Nate with them, something her son had been thrilled about. "I miss both of you."

"I miss you, too, baby," his voice had gone growly and rough, and made her grin. A different sound, this a masculine rumble. Connor laughed. "Coop says I'm hopeless in love. What do you think, honey?"

"Tell Coop he's the same for his wife, so that's okay." Head tipped to the side, trapping the phone on her shoulder, Jaime's hands kept moving, straightening the mail she'd just pulled from her purse, gathered a few minutes ago from the box in the lobby. An envelope slipped out, and she glanced down, fingers about to tuck it back into place when she saw the return address. A college in New England. Connor laughed while she tugged it free from the pile, turning it over and over in her hands. "Connor, honey?" He quietened and then made an interrogatory sound. "There's a letter here for Nate."

"The school we talked about?" She nodded, then realized he couldn't see her.

"Yeah."

"Open it, baby."

"What if they don't...?" Jaime's voice trailed off, because this was something she wanted for Nate. The principal had called her in for a conference a month ago, and she'd taken Connor with her. *Like I could have left him at home*, she thought, shaking her head in amusement at the idea. But he'd proven a good addition to the meeting, because he knew just the right questions to ask.

"Nate is the most extraordinary young man I've ever had the pleasure to instruct."

That had been the opening statement, and had taken Jaime's breath away.

"His intellect is immense, and it comes with a grounded sense of self that isn't present in many prodigies his age. Miss Grimes,"—Mr. Paterson leaned forwards, elbows on the desk—"I've taken him as far as I can."

"You mean this year, right?" She knew Nate had jumped topics and subjects frequently in the past months, seeming to breeze through the work assigned to him. "You'll have different classes in the fall?"

"No, Miss Grimes. I mean he has circumnavigated the entire high school class catalog. He has either completed or tested out of every class needed to graduate with an honors diploma." Connor made a noise and the man turned to look at him. "He's amazing to work with, and I will be the poorer for losing the interaction with him on a daily basis."

"I don't understand." Jaime was near tears because this man had seemed willing to help Nate, had gotten their hopes up for the year, and had come through on those promises. Until now. "He's ten, just ten years old. Where will Nate go, if not with you?"

"Miss Grimes, has he talked about college with you? He took home a folder of paperwork a few weeks ago. When we didn't receive it back, I assumed you were making alternative arrangements for his continued studies." Jaime shook her head, and Connor's hand closed around hers. "Academically, he's ready for college. Emotionally, well, that will be up to you. Based on his work this year, I entered his name for the Donohue Scholar Award, and he is one of two finalists. While we

can be assured he will receive ample scholarship offers, that award is more than forty-thousand dollars for the runner-up. Miss Grimes, Nate can go wherever he decides to go next year."

Jaime traced her finger along the top edge of the envelope. "I'll wait for Nate," she whispered.

"Okay, baby." Connor's voice was just as soft. "We'll see you tomorrow."

"See you tomorrow."

More noise from the background and she heard the truck door open and close, then Connor's voice. "How much do you love me?"

"More than you'll ever know," she assured him with a smile, hoping the warmth of it echoed through her words. "More than you'll ever know."

The call disconnected and Jaime laid the phone on the table. Carefully she placed the envelope on top of the stack, lining up the corners and edges. *We're moving in with Connor*, she told herself, and smiled.

Connor

Wrench gripped in one hand, Connor wormed his way underneath the tractor, looking up at the grease and hydraulic fluid caking the front end. "You'd think there'd be an easier way to bleed the line," he complained, pressing one heel into the dirt and shoving hard, trying to get another few inches underneath. "Damn thing shouldn't take two people."

A grunt, then he saw movement above him as Cooper got into position. "Ready."

Connor reached up and used the wrench to open the petcock, growling when nothing emitted from the nozzle directly underneath. "Nothing yet." Cooper moved and grunted, then a drop of fluid appeared. "No go, no flow." Cooper shifted again, and there was a spitting sound, then a hiss, then a sputter of fluid. "Pump it one more time." Cooper changed position, and Connor saw his shadow on the floor shift in response, thrown there by the sunset. Tonight would be the last on the farm, and they'd all be headed back to Memphis in the morning. Another sputter above him, and then he watched a steady drip of fluid, waiting a few moments to be sure all the air was gone from the line before he tightened the valve again. "Done."

He was crawling, working his way out from under the tractor, reversing the previous process when two hands gripped his ankles and he was dragged feet first out from under the tractor. His shirt rucked up in the back, gathering dirt and stalks of hay into his waistband. "Asshole," he called, the thread of anger in his voice bright and hard when Cooper bent over him, laughing, holding out one hand. Connor reluctantly gripped the offered hand and let his brother pull him to his feet. They joked and laughed for a minute more, then Connor looked out the barn door to where Nate had Sam by the hand, walking the smaller boy towards the pen where the bottle calves were. He swallowed hard, imagining for a moment that Nate walked hand in hand with a little brother, one that he and Jaime gave the boy.

"What's that look for, baby bro?" Cooper's hand fell on his shoulder, fingers gripping hard. "Something wrong?"

Connor shook his head. No way could he tell his brother what he'd been thinking. Ever since Jaime had been at the hospital, he'd been holding his breath hoping no one would see what was in his heart. Since the first time he'd felt the baby move, Connor had been jealous and angry. Angry at Cooper and Marie, because the child Jaime was carrying wasn't his, couldn't be his. Bought and paid for, an agreement he'd promised long ago, not understanding how life could change a man's view.

He couldn't say anything to Jaime, because she was intent on this, still. Even after the scare with the bleeding, she'd just kicked in and done everything the doctors recommended, waiting it out. Now she was a month away from having the baby, and she'd be going home from the hospital with empty arms, while Marie and Cooper would take his...

Connor shook his head, hard, trying to force the idea away.

"I love you, you know that, right?" Cooper's announcement was a surprise and pulled Connor's eyes to him, seeing an understanding that broke his heart. "Come on, tell me. Use your words." That made Connor drop his chin as it was something their father told them often. "Can't fix what I don't know."

"You ever wonder what if? What if I'd met Jaime a month before?" Connor shook his head, looking at Nate and Sam again, watching as the older boy helped Sam climb up a single rung on the fence, leaning through so he could scratch the heads of the calves that jostled around, eager for affection. "What if she weren't doing this?"

"We'd have found a different surrogate." Cooper's statement was so matter-of-fact it stunned Connor. "Marie and I have had conversations along the same lines." He stepped closer, wrapping an arm around Connor's shoulders. "Many conversations. The two of you just fit so well. There isn't anything you're thinking that she and I haven't already talked through."

Connor shook his head. "No, you don't know what I'm thinking." *You'd have a shitfit if you did, because of the money and time. And Marie would be devastated, which means even if I could talk about it, there's no way Jaime would do that to her.* "No idea."

"Connor, the woman you love is carrying your baby." Seems Cooper *could* know what he'd been thinking. "Something that felt so right at the beginning, doesn't feel so right anymore." Cooper whispered, "We see it every time we're around you guys. And it doesn't feel right. Not to me, and not to Marie. We see how you are with her. Connor, you've been there for everything. Everything. Jaime loves you, and the only reason she's not dying inside is because she made an agreement, and that woman is loyal to the bone. I think we should have a sit-down conversation, the four of us, and see where we want to go from here. Because I can't take that from you, can't take this child."

Connor turned on his heel, staring at Cooper, not certain he'd heard correctly. Cooper smiled sadly, staring at Connor. "Kills, bro. Kills." Cooper swallowed, and Connor saw his eyes grow wet. "We want another kid. Want to give Sam what I had with you and Cole. Family. Things that matter. But what does it say to him if I ignore the feelings of one of the most important people in my life? Huh? What does that say about family? Marie and me, we've talked, trying to figure out how to bring it up without seeming like assholes. This isn't something that can be just allowed to rock on, like nothing was wrong. As much as it kills me to say this, it would haunt you every day of your life, for the rest of your life. You're my brother. I can't."

Connor's eyes closed slowly, and he bit back his first reaction of denial. Cooper knew him too well. "But you and Marie—"

"We'll find a way. It'll just be a different way." Cooper squeezed hard and Connor opened his eyes, blinking fast against the wet that smeared his vision. "You've got to talk to her, man. Make sure you're on the same page. There's not much time to sort it out, but we can do anything we need, Connor."

Chapter Eighteen
Jaime

Her eyes filled with tears. She kept her gaze pointed out the window, steadfastly not looking at Connor. *No, he can't mean it.* She sniffed and swallowed a sob, then pulled in a breath that broke in a half a dozen places. "Baby," he murmured, and she heard him moving, coming towards where she stood. Reflexively she lifted one hand, palm out to him in an unmistakable "stop" motion. What he had voiced was something she refused to think about. Had been pushing down the feelings of loss every time she went to Marie's and saw the nursery setup. She'd not allowed herself to think anything other than the reason she'd set out on this journey. The purpose of the path they'd been following.

Shaking her head, she choked out, "Don't. Don't say that. I can't." If she ever once allowed herself to think the

211

phrase "my baby," she knew she wouldn't be able to follow through with this.

"Listen to me, Jaime." Ignoring her hand, he moved closer. "Just listen, please. *God*, please."

"Connor, you of all people know what's at stake here. You know what we all went through to get to this place. You were part of what they went through to get Sam. You can't do this to them. *I* can't do this to them." Her voice broke again, and she sobbed, clawing control back painfully, her chest hitching and throat closing tightly around her words for a moment. "Don't do this to me."

"I'm not going to stop talking, honey. I'm not. Coop and me, we talked it out. He called Marie, and she feels the same way. I know you." Connor crooned the words, and she felt the first brush of his fingers across her cheeks. "I know you love me." She nodded and turned, burying her face against his chest.

He sighed deeply, relaxing in a way she couldn't mistake. He wasn't as certain of himself as he wanted her to think.

"I know, baby. I know you love me. And you love Marie, too. Even Coop, asshole he can be, you love him. And we did go through a lot. We've been through so much. But, honey…" His fingers were again grazing across her cheeks, sweeping the flood of tears away. His mouth teased along hers, then his lips were placed at her ear, and he whispered, "That's my baby. Our baby. Ours. I want you, and I want Nate, and I want to have this baby with you."

She sobbed harder, winding her arms around his neck, holding on tightly.

"Coop knew, even before I did. He knew, and so did Marie. They've been battling with it, trying to decide what to do. You and me, we're a unique case. I love you. Didn't plan on it, didn't plan for it. Never expected it. But I love you so much. And Coop said he couldn't do it, so we'll figure out something. Figure out a way. If you tell me you're with me, then we'll figure out a way."

Jaime

"I did not anticipate this."

Jaime looked up at the words to see a somber Sarah staring at her across the desk. "I'm sorry." Her words sounded so inadequate, and she winced, turning to look down at the toes of her shoes.

"We'll work out a way for the repayment of the monies already transferred to you—"

Connor interrupted, his arm settling around Jaime's shoulders. "I have that covered." Jaime shook her head. This was something they'd argued about, but he was adamant and she had gracefully given in. It felt as if she were still coming to grips with the idea that he wanted this with her, wanted this so much he was willing to do whatever was necessary.

Even now, she could scarcely believe this was happening. Everything had moved along so quickly after Connor came back from the family farm. They'd talked, then she'd called Marie who had already been crying, and Jaime had sobbed along with her after finding out Marie was shedding tears in relief that the uncertainty was over. Something Jaime didn't even know the couple had been dealing with, and realized they had such a deep love for Connor to consider doing this.

"The Thompsons aren't assured of another surrogate, but they have voluntarily released you from the agreement, Jaime."

She nodded. "I know."

Sarah stood, hand outstretched, "I wish you well, Jaime." They shook, and Sarah extended her arm again, and as Connor took it, she said, "You've made a hard decision. But seeing you together, I can't help but believe it's the right one. I wish all of you well." She smiled as she opened the door. "I expect some pictures. That's still our baby."

Connor put his hand on the small of Jaime's back, five blistering points of pressure as he guided her out the door. "We will," he promised. Then they were through the waiting room and outside. "Jaime, are you okay?" She nodded, feeling tears welling in her eyes again. "Can I...there's something I wanted to do. I've wanted to do more than anything." Jaime lifted her gaze, looking at his face through a watery haze. Before she could react, he was on one knee in front of her, one hand clutching at hers. "Jaime Grimes. Will you marry me?"

She stared down at him for a moment, long enough to see his mouth twist to the side. Long enough to see fear flash through his eyes and then she was crying and laughing, tugging on his hand to pull him awkwardly to his feet so she could wrap her arms around him. "Ring, soon as we get home," he murmured as he kissed her, long, slow, and deep.

Nate stared at her, a dark frown on his face. "You…" He swallowed. "For reals?"

Jaime nodded, holding Nate's eyes with her own. Connor was behind her, arms around her middle, hands cradling either side of her belly. He'd been in almost the same position since they'd gotten home from the clinic, elated that he didn't have to deny himself these experiences any longer. She hadn't realized how much they were both holding back with this pregnancy. Out of necessity at the time, but now that he didn't have to censor himself, Connor seemed nearly giddy with excitement.

Nate broke their shared gaze, and he cut a quick glance up to Connor's face. Whatever he saw there reassured him and when her boy looked at her face again, he did it with the broadest smile she'd ever seen on him. "Keeping the baby." She nodded. He pointed to her hand where Connor had parked a beautiful band with an understated diamond. Perfect for her, and she thought the fact he knew her so well boded well for their relationship. "Gonna get married." She nodded again. "What'd Uncle Jakey say?"

Jaime bit her lip and shook her head and admitted, "I haven't called him yet."

Nate hooted with laughter, falling off the arm of the couch where he'd perched when she'd called him in for a chat, landing on the seat cushions. "He's gonna have a fun time sorting this out."

Connor called to Nate, softly, but insistently, "Nate, your mom's gonna need you to say what you think, bud."

Nate popped up off the couch, standing beside the coffee table, looking at them with an intensity that made her unaccustomedly anxious. "You know I'm not an idiot, right?" Jaime took a breath and nodded, feeling Connor's chin bumping her shoulder as he nodded, too. "Mom, I think the two of you were the only ones who weren't expecting this at some point. Even Jordan knew. We talked about it the last time I tutored him. That"—he pointed to her belly and Connor's hands moved to cover her protectively—"is your baby, you and Coach. Uncle Coop"—*when did he start thinking of Cooper as his uncle?*—"knew a long time ago. Told me to watch out for you if Coach didn't get his thumb out of it."

At the glare she directed his way, he held up his hands, shaking his head. "Hey, I didn't say it. I just was repeating what he said."

"But what do you think, buddy?" Connor pushed, and she was glad of it because she was too afraid to know for certain.

"It's your baby, Coach." Nate shook his head. "Science explains so much with technical and chemical information, genetics and chromosomes, hereditary traits. When I say it's your baby, I don't mean it was your sperm that fertilized one of Mom's eggs. I mean, I totally understand what's involved with IVF, but that's not what I mean. This—" He gestured to the two of them standing so close. "—all of this. That's what I mean. You'd die before you let anything hurt her, or the baby." Nate paused and swallowed hard, then continued, "Or me. That's your baby, and we're your family. This—" He whirled his hand, indicating the three of them. "—makes sense to me. Count me in."

After dinner, Connor got her attention and tossed a cell phone to her, grinning when she fumbled the catch, finally trapping the phone against her belly. "Call your brother, honey."

She and Jacob had talked nearly every week during the pregnancy, and he was the only one she had felt comfortable voicing her misgivings to as things progressed with Connor. Not about the relationship, because that had been as easy and natural from the beginning as breathing. No, when she began to struggle against personalizing the pregnancy, he was the one she talked to. When she cried herself to sleep because of how sweet Connor was with Nate, and wanting that for her son, but more, wanting that for this baby, Jacob was who she called.

She pushed up from the couch, struggling to the edge of the cushion before she was able to climb to her feet. Pointing at the bedroom, she waited for Connor to nod before she went into the semi-darkened room and closed the door behind her.

Two rings and she heard, "My most beautiful sister in the whole world, how is that belly of yours, beautiful?"

Jaime grinned, recognizing this over the top greeting. "Trent. How are you?" She sank to the edge of the mattress, leaning back on one arm in the bed.

"Better than most, doll. You want to talk to your brudder?"

"I do, if he's handy." She smiled at Trent's laughter.

"Oh, he's handsy, all right. Allllll night long."

His exaggerated sing-song made her laugh, and she told him, "Ah, Jesus, Trenty. TMI."

The laughter caused a tendon along one side of her belly to twinge with pain, and Trent must have heard the catch in her breathing, because he asked, "All okay, beautiful?"

"Yeah. I mean, I think so." Huffing out a soft laugh, she corrected herself. "Yes, everything is okay. Better than okay, but I need to talk to Jacob and then he can tell you, okay?"

"Jakey," Trent yelled, mouth slightly away from the phone because the volume wasn't quite earsplitting. "Jakey, get a move on it. Baby sister has news and she won't share." Louder and higher pitched, his next yell caused her to pull the phone away from her ear. "Jakey. Now, honeybuns."

"Jesus," she heard Jacob in the background, "what's going on, babe?"

"Jaime's—" That was all Trent got out before Jacob's voice was coming through the speaker.

"Is Jaime okay? Connor? Nate?" He sounded so frightened it tore a piece from her heart. Nate had called him the night she'd been bleeding, and then he'd talked to Connor afterwards, but for several hours her big brother didn't know much, except he was hours and hours away from her and she needed someone. It sounded like he hadn't given up that fear yet, so she rushed to reassure him.

"Uh, yeah, last time I checked Jaime's okay. Dork, everything's fine. I'm sitting on my bed, lounging like a big lizard." She went down on her back, levering herself to one side, curling her legs up onto the mattress. "How's my favorite turd?"

"God, don't do that to me, woman. You're the scary, reproducing one. You sure you're okay?"

"Yeah, all okay. I have weekly visits with the OB now, just because we're kind of on countdown. Four weeks to go." Closing her eyes, she let the sound of Jacob's voice roll over her, calming her.

"Sounds good, James. Really good. So everything looks to be on track with the baby? How's Nate doing?" *Jacob's good*, she thought, plugging the sentence with a question, then a segue in case talking about the baby was too hard.

"Everything is right on track. And Nate's good. But I called to tell you something." She cleared her throat, suddenly nervous again.

"So I gathered from the way Trent is hovering, waiting not so patiently. You...are you sure you're okay?" Now he sounded suspicious again, and she grinned.

"How do you feel about being an uncle again?" Jacob was silent, and she rushed to fill the gap. "To this baby, I mean. What do you think about being Uncle Jakey?" He was quiet, and she could hear Trent in the background, the rumbling murmur of his voice counterpoint for Jacob's silence. "Jacob?"

"How are you handling Marie and Cooper?" Jacob cut to the chase, just like he always did, his insight stunning her. "You've become friends with them, are they gonna...that friendship, honey. That's Connor's brother. Can you do this to them?"

"It was their idea, sort of. I mean, Cooper brought it up to Connor. I hadn't said anything, wouldn't let myself. But they saw how Connor was, and how I felt, even without me saying a word. I think this is..." She let her voice trail off, not sure how to convey what she felt. "It's hard, Jacob. I think it's...for the best sounds wrong, like this baby would be a burden, and it absolutely wouldn't be. We both love it so much. This is what I needed." She cradled her belly in one arm, the other holding the phone to her ear. "I love this baby with all my heart. Knowing it's part of Connor and me, and it's just...perfect." The last word was a barely-there whisper, and she held her breath, waiting.

"With your whole heart." Jacob sighed, the sound so filled with happiness for her that she couldn't hold back the tears. "Like you do everything. You're all-in, James. You're gonna be Connor's baby momma."

In the background Trent yelled, "Oh. My. *God!* Tickets, we need tickets. God, Jakey, we've missed out on nearly everything." Closer to the phone there was a grunt and then the sounds of a scuffle, then Trent was on the call. "Sweet girl, tell me you haven't had a baby shower without me. Do not dare. Now, here's your brother, and I want you to tell him everything. We love you."

"Love you, too, Trent." A pause, and she waited a moment, then said, "Jacob?" He hummed in her ear, and she said, "I'm so happy. Connor is everything I ever wanted in someone to love, and to love me. He's really good with Nate, too." She gasped, remembering Nate's acceptance letter they had celebrated and said, "Oh, Nate. He's got news of his own. I'll let him tell you, but it's really good. So good. I couldn't have done this for him without Connor. It's like every good thing in our lives in the past year have been tied up in Connor. I really do love him."

"I'm glad, Jaime. You've always deserved so much. I'm glad you're finally getting everything."

She smiled and settled back, head on the pillow, and chatted with her big brother.

Connor

Parking the truck in the school lot, Connor swung out and slammed the door behind him. Long strides took him to the school where he saw an agitated-looking Nate staring out a window in the office. Even before he got the door open, he could hear the boy's calls of, "Coach, Coach!"

The principal hadn't told Connor what was going on, just called him out of practice to come to Nate's school immediately. As soon as Jaime and Nate had officially moved into the apartment with him, Connor and Jaime had put him on Nate's emergency contacts, which meant if they couldn't get Jaime this morning, they would've called him.

"Paterson, what's going on?" Connor stopped inside the office, letting Nate come to him and the boy did, wrapping him up in a hard hug. "Buddy, you okay?" He cradled the back of Nate's head, remembering again that the kid was so young. Only ten, no matter how intelligent he was.

"Nate wanted to be the first to tell you." Paterson stepped out, pulling the door closed behind him, giving Connor privacy with his soon-to-be stepson.

"Tell me what, bud?"

Nate took a deep breath and squeezed him, then relaxed slightly, leaning back and looking up at Connor's face. "I won."

Won? What game is he talking about? "Buddy?" Nate's eyes were shining, and he had a piece of paper crumpled in one hand. Connor took a guess. "The scholarship? The Donohue?" His gut clenched; that single award would set Nate up for his academic career, and open doors far beyond the two college acceptance letters they'd already received. Everyone would want to have Nate on their campus now. "You won?" Nate nodded, eyes gleaming with excitement. "Nathan, that's amazing!" He wrapped his arms around the boy. "So proud of you, son." Nate burrowed against him, shaking with excitement.

Chapter Nineteen

Connor

"Bro." Connor grinned when he answered the phone, Cooper never seemed to grow out of the teenaged greeting. "Got an idea. Wanted to run it past you."

"Hit me." Connor signaled to one of his assistants, waiting for him to nod before Connor stepped back, turning his attention to the phone and away from keeping two-dozen testosterone driven boys from killing each other. "What's up?"

"We had four, do you remember? Embryos? We implanted two, kept two on ice." Connor's throat tightened, because even in all the excitement he and Jaime were having, setting up a nursery on short notice, and packing eight-months' worth of anticipation and excitement into four short weeks, he hadn't lost sight of how much Cooper and Marie had given up.

"Yeah, I remember. There were four good ones, and you decided to take two, leaving two for the next try if needed." He shook his head. "Didn't think we'd be the cause of you needing them. Not like this."

"Bro, this isn't me raggin' on you. This is me having an epiphany." Cooper laughed, and the fist clutching Connor's chest loosened slightly. The intensity in Cooper's voice grew, deepened as he said, "We have two." Silence for a beat, then Cooper said, "The clinic sent a profile over. A gestational carrier."

"That's amazing, Coop. I'm so glad. God." He laughed, lighter than he'd been in days. "That's…amazing."

"Small snag." His brother sounded unsure, quiet. "Those baby-cicles? They aren't ours. Me and Marie. Releasing Jaime from the contract left them in limbo. They would have gotten in touch with her eventually, because they are hers. Murky waters, Connor."

"Can she, can we give…is it like a donated egg? Can we do that?" He laughed, but the sound was tight and hard. "Let me call Jaime. Make sure I'm not overstepping, but I can guarantee you that any babies we want to make after this one are going to be done the fun way. She doesn't need IVF, so those…let me call Jaime. I'll call you right back."

Two minutes passed and he was back on the phone with his brother. "One or both, whatever you need, brother. She's thrilled. This is a good thing."

"A very good thing," Cooper said quietly. "We'll go with one. See if we get a sticky one. Are you sure? This...biologically it's no different from the baby Jaime's carrying now."

"Totally different, Coop, and you know it." Connor didn't have to hesitate, didn't have to think as this was the core of what had been killing him about the baby. "The baby in her belly is mine, because I love her. It's mine because I was there. And yes, it's mine because it's my jizz and her egg, but it's about the experience. That—" He paused, and grinned. "—baby-cicle, as you called it, that's a chance for you and Marie to get what you need. Genetics aside, that's not my baby. This, the field goal kicker who wakes me up at night? That's my kid."

Crawling into bed behind Jaime that night, Connor gently kissed the nape of her neck, moving her hair to one side so he could nibble and press a series of kisses there. She arched her back, pushing into him with a nearly-silent groan. She'd already been in bed when he got home; the practice had gone long as he and his assistants watched footage after the kids had left. "Hey, baby. I didn't mean to wake you."

"Mmmm," she hummed and shifted, then groaned. "I gotta pee anyway." She shuffled sideways, working to the edge of the mattress and then rolled to a sitting position. "You know, they said this baby is normal sized. I think they lied. It's huge. Ginormous." She pushed up and stood, twisting back to grin at him. "Especially when it's dancing on my bladder. So sexy. Sexy, smexy times."

Connor laughed softly. "Come back to bed, baby. Go pee and come back to me."

He was dozing when the mattress jostled, waking him. "Hey. What took you so long?"

"I had a false start. A couple of them." She giggled. "Pee, stand up. Sit down. Pee. It's like the pee calisthenics." He rolled to his back, letting her arrange herself alongside him, head to his shoulder, her arm across his gut. "How was practice?"

"Good, kids are doing well. I'm going to be glad to get this tourney behind us." After the upcoming weekend, he didn't have anything to take him out of town until after the baby was due. "How's my boy doing tonight?"

"You don't know it's a boy." Her tone was half-teasing and half-annoyed, because this was the only bone of contention between them. The OB knew the gender, and that information had been released to Cooper and Marie as part of the surrogate process, but Jaime didn't know. She'd decided that if she'd gone this long without knowing, then she needed to let nature do the reveal for them. Connor could have pushed her, but he liked the soft look on her face when she talked about not knowing.

"And you don't know it's not."

"True," she said, and yawned, stretching her legs, tipping her hips with a groan. "Fake labor sucks."

She'd been dealing with what seemed like a lot of Braxton-Hicks contractions, assuring him they weren't painful, just annoying. But when she'd catch her breath as she stood, or stop and press a palm to the side of her belly when walking, it made him wince in sympathy, and worry. He'd remember the look on her face when he got to the ER the night she nearly miscarried, and have to remind himself not to panic.

"About the not knowing…" He trailed off when she tensed up. "I'm kidding, honey. You know that. We're doing this how you want. That's all that matters to me. You happy, healthy? The baby healthy? Everything that matters, right there."

She sighed. "I know. But you're kinda right. Names are harder not knowing."

"No, they aren't." He kept his words quiet, his tone soft, one hand gliding up her hip to coast along the side of her belly. He tapped gently. "We know there's a single kid in there." She giggled and nodded, her hair moving across his skin, and he took a deep breath, pulling in her scent. "We know it's a fifty-fifty that it's a girl or boy. We have one of those, so we pick two names. Two names, not too hard."

"Four names, two first, two middle." She yawned again. "Matilda."

With a headshake, he offered, "Mildred."

"Natalie."

The word resonated with him, sounding enough like Nate's name to make it clear there was a sibling connection. Like with him and Cooper, and Cole. When he didn't come back with a different suggestion, she tipped her chin up and looked at him. Connor held his breath, then said, "I like Natalie."

"Natalie as a first or middle? I like middle."

"I like it as a first." He pulled in a breath. "Natalie Marie."

"Oh, I like that." Her voice was soft and intense, nearly quivering with her delight. "I like that one. Put a pin in it."

Connor laughed softly. "Okay, we have the pink brigade nailed." He paused a minute, then said, "For our boy, what do you think about Benjamin?"

"Everett." Connor made a horrified noise, and she laughed, halfway between a snort and a giggle, which made him laugh in turn. "Okay, not Everett."

"No, definitely not Everett. Doesn't go with Thompson. Nicholas." She shook her head, so he tried again. "Matthew?"

"Matthew Cole," she said without hesitation, and he found his breath frozen in his chest. "What do you think?" When he didn't respond, she adjusted so she could see his face in the dark. "Connor?"

"Connor's taken," he choked out the bad joke, and she ignored it, focused on him.

"Connor, I'm sorry, honey." Settling back in beside him, she seemed prepared to keep the game going, but he lifted a hand to cup her chin, bringing her mouth to his.

"I like Matthew Cole, honey. Natalie Marie Thompson, or Matthew Cole Thompson. Our baby's got a name." He kissed her again, then gave her a squeeze. "Sleep, Jaime. Love you."

A quiet, satisfied-sounding sigh, then she said, "I love you, too, Connor."

"Would you be okay if I talked to Nate about adopting him?" She froze against him, not even breathing. He'd just soothed her, hoping she'd go to sleep and then dropped that bomb on her. Connor shook his head. *I can be such an ass.* "Are you okay with the idea?" She hadn't talked about Nate's father much, but Grimes wasn't his last name; it was her maiden name.

"Is that something you want, Connor?" Her question was worded carefully, keeping any personal investment in the idea out of the equation.

"Yes," he answered, and left it there.

"Are you certain?"

"Yes," he repeated, holding the line on his firmness, not letting any give enter the word.

"Then yes, talk to Nate."

Jaime

Her phone rang and Jaime looked at the display, feeling a lightness in her chest when she saw the caller's information. "Marie," she said when she answered, "I'm so glad the embryos are good." Everything had moved fast on that front, and their carrier had been implanted yesterday. Cooper had called Connor with the good news last night. "How are you feeling about this go around?"

"Good, really good. She's carried before, and she's just twenty-six. We used one, leaving one in the bank just in case. I'm excited." Marie sounded it and Jaime smiled. The noise level changed on the call, and Jaime heard Sam in the background, laughing. "We're headed to the park. Want to meet us there?"

Jaime wrinkled her nose, looking around the apartment at the stack of boxes in the corner of the dining room. Jacob had sent all of his and Trent's baby gift purchases to her address with the stern instructions that she wasn't to open any of them. He and Trent would be coming in this weekend and staying at a local hotel for a few days, and Trent had been busily planning a baby shower and wedding. The clutter was making her crazy, plus she couldn't avoid knowing what some of the gifts were, since they were mailed in the manufacturer's original box, which made her itch to open boxes. "I'd love to, but I have a lot to do here. Nate and Connor are at the tournament and won't be home until tomorrow, so I have a narrow window of male-free nesting I can do."

231

At first, when the two couples had come to the mutual agreement that the surrogacy wasn't going to happen, she'd felt odd saying things like that around Marie. It had taken her friend sitting her down and making her listen to show Jaime that there truly was no resentment about the decision. Marie was as happy for her as any friend and soon-to-be sister-in-law could be, as supportive as Jaime could have wished for. Now, when she had thoughts about the pregnancy, she didn't try and censor herself.

"He left you there by yourself?" Marie sounded scandalized, as if Connor had gone out clubbing while Jaime stayed home, and the idea of that made her roll her eyes. "You're getting married next week! You're pregnant! What was he thinking?"

"Uh, that I needed him not in my face asking me every two minutes if I was okay? I swear, he's freaked out about the Braxton-Hicks more than I am. Way more. I keep remembering what you said about when you were having Sam, how he nearly got sick at the video." Jaime laughed. "I haven't brought it up to him, but what if he faints during delivery?"

Marie joined in on the laughter, and Jaime heard Sam laughing in the background, chortling along without knowing why. "Oh my God, he'll never live it down. You need to talk about it. Pretend you want to have a plan in case he goes down." Jaime laughed harder, and then winced as one of the warm-up contractions hit, a tiny pinching pain just under her ribs.

"You and Sam have fun at the park. I'll see you at the shower if not before, right?" Trent had enlisted Marie to help with the party, and she had jumped at the chance with a quickness that made Jaime's heart swell with love.

"Wouldn't miss it, Jaime." Voice slightly away from the phone, she called to Sam, "Tell Aunt Jaime you love her." Then she joined in with her son, both singing the words, "We love you, Aunt Jaime." Marie came back to the phone and echoed the words again. "Love you, Jaime."

"Love you, too, Marie."

Standing just outside the security area at the airport, Jaime shifted from foot to foot, trying to ignore what her body was telling her. According to the arrival boards, Jacob and Trent's plane had just landed, and she wanted her face to be the first thing he saw when he came down the escalator. Jacob and Trent were renting a car and had tried to tell her she didn't need to meet them at the airport, but there was no way she would let her brother fly all the way to see her and not be here when he arrived.

Crap. A particularly hard push against her bladder made her hang her head in defeat. "Nate, stay right here. If I'm not back, then the responsibility of greeting your uncles lands on your shoulders." Nate grinned up at her, and she laughed, then bit her lip when that proved unwise. Twisting her neck, she looked up at Connor, reaching up to cover one of his hands where it rested on her shoulders. "Your child needs me to pee."

As always happened when she made a reference like that, an expression of joy and pleasure rolled across his features. He dipped his head, brushing her mouth with his and murmured, "Then go pee, baby momma."

Jaime walked away at a far more sedate pace than she would have preferred, but she'd learned that rapid waddling and urgency like this were not a good combination. On her way back, the crowds were thicker, and she had to stop more than once to let the flow of people move around her, waiting for a space big enough for her belly. Over the heads of the passengers making their way to baggage claim, she saw Connor, and then right next to him her brother. "Jacob," she shrieked, watching as both their heads turned towards her, then Jacob was moving, coming to her, and then wrapped his arms around her.

They stood like that for a minute, Jaime absorbing the feel of her brother, not even trying to beat back the tears that overflowed her eyes. When she sniffed in his ear, she felt him start to shake and knew it for laughter. "Do not snot on me, James," he ordered, giving her a squeeze before setting her away from him. "So beautiful." His eyes were shining, and she knew she wasn't the only one overwhelmed by the reunion.

"Oh. My. God. What a gorgeous belly. Jaime, honey, your belly is gorgeous." Before she could respond, Trent was crouched down in front of her, a hand on either side of her rounded abdomen, crooning softly. "You're gonna be so loved, little munchkin. Surrounded by love." He rose and gently pushed Jacob's hands out of the way, pulling her in for a hug. For all he sounded like a goofball sometimes, Jacob's husband was big and burly, with broad shoulders that belied his job sitting at a computer all day. Brushing her cheek with a kiss, he whispered, "So happy to be here, beautiful."

In the background she heard Nate's voice, rapidly recounting all the things that had happened since the last time they'd seen Jacob. He sounded happy, and when Connor's arm circled her shoulders, she sighed and leaned into him. "We're glad you're here too, Trent. Did you meet Connor?" Looking up, she caught Connor's nod and smiled.

At Cooper and Marie's for dinner that night, the three couples sat around the dining room table, laughing and sharing stories. Trent and Marie had become fast friends, using the past week to bond over Skype and the upcoming baby shower, so when Marie had offered to host the group for a meal, Jaime hadn't hesitated. She knew Jacob still had reservations about the entire situation and was worried Cooper would resent Connor and Jaime's decision. Family was important to Jacob, and the idea that the two brothers might be divided bothered him. She had hoped seeing them together like this would help lay all his doubts to rest.

Nate and Sam were in the backyard chasing lightning bugs, Nate the keeper of the jar and lid, Sam bringing them to him one at a time. Through the open windows, she could hear Nate explaining the chemistry behind the glowing bugs. "...luciferin is also being used to help with brain imagery, and there's some discussion about how it can be used to track trace chemicals that attach themselves to tumors. What if that firefly you have right now is the cure for cancer, Sammy? What if?"

She focused back in on the conversation around her and noticed Jacob staring at her with a funny expression on his face. "What?" she mouthed, lifting her eyebrows. Biting his lip, he shook his head and leaned over to whisper into Trent's ear. She couldn't hear him, but the way Trent's face softened, it had to be something sweet and the idea that Jacob had this kind of love in his life made her smile. Trent flicked a glance at her, then her belly, then he turned to Jacob and cupped his palm around her brother's jaw, tracing across Jacob's lips with the tip of his thumb. *Now I gotta know.* "What are you whispering about over there?"

Trent answered for them, not breaking the connection with Jacob. "My husband wants a baby."

Jaime sucked in a breath and then turned, burying her face into Connor's neck. He wrapped his arms around her as Cooper and Marie congratulated the couple. "Honey," Connor murmured to her, shifting and pulling her so she was perched sideways on his lap, "why are you crying?"

Jaime shook her head, not wanting to admit she'd had a lingering fear that their decision to keep the baby might negatively impact her brother. When she first called Jacob to explore the idea of being a surrogate, he had sounded so wistful, she knew a child was something he wanted, but the stories about women doing what she'd done and backing out at the last minute had put him off the idea. For him to be openly considering it now, sitting here in the home of the couple who had started her down this path to being with Connor, was no less than miraculous. Whispering, trying to keep her voice steady, she said, "I'm just happy, Con."

Then Marie laughed, clapping her hands together smartly as she said, "Wine for most of us, water for the rotund one." Jaime untucked her head and stuck her tongue out at Marie, wrinkling her nose as she tried not to smile. Marie had turned towards the kitchen when she suddenly whirled, eyes wide, and blurted, "Hey, Jacob, what if you guys were able to take Jaime's last embryo? Our carrier is pregnant, we just found out today, which means we hopefully won't need that one." Stunned silence settled on the room, and Jaime stared at Marie, who was now standing with both hands over her mouth. "Okay, that just got weird. Sorry." She shook her head and laughed again. "Definitely need wine."

Jaime was frozen, her heart pounding hard. The idea of Jacob and Trent with a baby was amazing, and the idea that she might be the one to help them was even more so.

Trent spoke, his words coming slowly as he turned from Jacob to stare at Jaime. "We'll need to talk...like a lot. But, something along those lines is an idea with merit," he said. "One of the things our friends struggle with is whether to try and keep a genetic link. And if they do, then with who. Family matters, we all know that, but

I don't think it matters as much as love. Lots to talk about. Marie, using that particular embryo might be too weird, but"—he winked at Jaime—"keeping an egg in the family could actually be kind of genius." Jaime twisted and planted her face back into Connor's neck, feeling and hearing the rumble of his laughter.

Chapter Twenty

Connor

"I didn't think today would ever come," Cooper said, leaning in and fiddling with Connor's collar, straightening his tie slightly. "Glad you decided to make an honest woman out of her before your dau...I mean child comes." Connor rolled his eyes. Cooper had been making the same jokes about the baby's gender for the past month. He'd start to say son or daughter, boy or girl, then comically correct himself. Well, Cooper thought it was funny at least.

"Did Marie say if Jaime's ready?" Cooper had just gotten off the phone with his wife, who was in a room down the hall with Jaime, performing much the same role. "How long?"

Cooper stepped back and stared at Connor. "They'll be ready as soon as I call."

"Then call, man. What's the hold-up?" Connor started towards the door, stopping when Cooper's hand landed on his arm. "What?" A bolt of fear shot through him. "What's wrong?" He knew she wouldn't be changing her mind, not Jaime. *She loves me. What if it's the baby?* "What's wrong with the baby?"

"Nothing's wrong with the baby. And Jaime's just fine. I wanted to…I just wanted to say something to you. That's all." Cooper looked slightly hangdog at Connor's fear, and that allowed him to settle back on his heels, waiting. "I love you. You know it. We don't say it much, but we should. We know how fast things can go wrong. How shit can happen when you don't even see it coming. I worried about you, bro. When we lost Cole, you were gone, man. For a long time, you were lost, too. Breathing and walking around, but so far gone from us it didn't seem like we'd ever get you back. Jaime—" Cooper paused and shook his head. "Jaime got you started on the path back to us. Jaime and Nate. This baby."

He sighed. "Do you know why I've never had doubts about what we all decided? Because I'd have given anything to have my baby brother back, and Jaime was the catalyst. Everything she brings to the table, helped bring you home. I love you, bro."

Connor stared at him, wordless, fighting through familiar stifling emotions of guilt and loss, grief and sorrow. He stepped forwards and wrapped his arms around Cooper's shoulders, leaning on his brother as he should have had the strength to do all along.

"Love you, Connor." Cooper's voice was thick with unshed tears. After a moment, the two men straightened, pounded each other on the back, and stepped backwards. Cooper smiled, and said, "Let's go get you hitched."

Standing at the front of the tiny country church his family attended in Sugarglide, Connor scanned the faces in the pews. Like him, they were waiting for the bride to come through the back door. Cooper stood beside him, and Marie would be standing up with Jaime. Trent had abandoned tradition and was seated next to Connor's parents on the groom's side of the church along with Nate. Her parents wouldn't be coming to visit separately until after the baby was born, and without hesitation, Jacob had agreed to escort his sister up the aisle. "It's all just perfect," Connor whispered, knowing Cooper could hear him.

The music started and his eyes flew to the doorway to see Marie standing there, smiling broadly. Cooper muttered, "Yeah," as his wife started walking towards them.

Then everything faded away and all Connor could see was Jaime. Wearing flats to accommodate her gait, she was gorgeous in the ivory skirt and jacket she'd picked for the wedding. "Totally Jaime," Jacob had said when he saw the outfit, noting it was practical and pretty, without being flashy. *Totally Jaime*, Connor agreed now.

When Nate stood to speak along with Jacob, telling the minister and everyone in the church that Jaime was

241

being given away by, "Her brother and I," while Jacob said, "Her son and I," Connor heard Jaime sniff, and leaned over to whisper, "No waterworks. You promised."

Eyes shining brightly, she smiled up at him and nodded. Then sniffed again as her lips quivered when she whispered back, "Hush, you. Hormones."

A few minutes later and he held her hand, sliding the wedding band to the base of her finger to rest alongside the engagement ring she never took off. He got to watch her solemn and focused expression as she repeated the words, "In sickness and in health, for richer or poorer, as long as we both shall live." Then, Connor finally got to kiss his wife. And, as he cradled her face in his hands, nibbling and gently caressing her lips with his, he felt the now-familiar push and kick from her belly. Pulling back, she smiled up at him. "I love you, Connor Thompson," Jaime mouthed the words, and he nodded.

"With my whole heart," he promised, and her eyes grew bright.

"Okay, Jaime, I need you to hold off. Don't push." The doctor sounded distracted, and Connor glanced at him, seeing his head bent as he focused on what was happening between Jaime's legs. "Breathe, okay? Hold off."

Connor renewed his grip on Jaime's hand, feeling her fingers wrap more tightly around his thumb. "No, no. I *need* to push." She sucked in a deep breath, and Connor got in her face, getting as close as he could, trying to get her attention.

"Jaime, don't push. Breathe." He panted those exaggerated puffs of air that had always felt slightly silly, until now at least. He'd seen how it worked for her, letting her manage her way through contractions that nearly shot off the graph paper that measured intensity. "Breathe. Don't push."

"I need to push," she wailed, but if she was talking that meant she wasn't bearing down. She took another deep breath, and Connor shook her hand. Teeth gritted, she ground out, "No. Please."

"In a minute, honey. Just a minute, breathe with me." Connor tried demonstrating the breathing again, but her face twisted and she squeezed her eyes shut on a rising cry.

"Okay, Jaime. Easy push. Slow and easy, tiny, tiny push." The doctor's orders came just in time, and Connor felt Jaime's hand lock down on his and with eyes clamped closed, she pushed. Her eyes popped open and she made a sound of surprise just as the doctor said, "It's a boy."

Jaime's eyes flew to Connor's. She looked as stunned as he felt.

Then she whispered, "Matthew Cole."

The doctor must have heard her, because he repeated, "Welcome to the world, Matthew Cole."

Jaime

Connor's voice called her up from sleep, and Jaime blinked, opening her eyes to see him near the windows of the hospital room. He was looking down at the bassinette, holding a phone to his ear. "Yeah, they're both perfect, Jacob. I should have waited for her to wake up, but I wanted you to know we're okay. Everyone's healthy. Ten fingers, ten toes, one nose." He paused, then nodded in agreement to whatever her brother was saying on the other end of the call. "He is, he's gorgeous. Matthew Cole." Another pause and Connor dropped one hand down, resting his palm on the blue blanket inside the bassinette. "Yeah, my brother's name. Your sister's amazing."

He lifted his head to look out the window and met her eyes in the reflection of the glass. "She's awake. Want to talk to her?" Two strides and he was at the side of the bed, bending to brush his lips across hers. "Jacob says he'd like to talk for a minute, if you're up to it?"

Staring up into his eyes, she pursed her lips demandingly, and he bent to kiss her more thoroughly before handing her the phone with a grin. "Jacob." Her voice sounded raspy to her own ears, and she swallowed hard, still feeling exhausted. "Did Connor send you a picture yet?"

"Not yet," Jacob responded, and she frowned up at Connor who shook his head. "I'm sure he will as soon as we get off the phone. I just wanted to talk to you and make sure everything's okay."

"He's perfect, Jakey." Connor was wheeling the bassinette over to the bed, and she shoved at the pillows, trying to arrange herself more comfortably so she could look over and see tiny Matthew. "Just under seven pounds, but he's long. His feet are so big, and his toes are prehensile." Jacob laughed. "That's what Nate said, anyway. I gathered that means he's got monkey feet." Connor picked up the bed controller, and Jaime felt the top part of the mattress moving, letting her sit more upright. "He's perfect."

"And so are you." Jacob's voice was warm with affection, and she could picture him smiling. "Trent said to tell you we love you, and if your hubby doesn't send pictures STAT, we'll be back in Memphis in a few hours to remedy the situation."

Jaime handed the phone back to Connor when they hung up, and he quickly took a picture of Matthew in the bassinette, then handed it back to her before he gathered the blanketed bundle into his arms. Grinning, she took several pictures before he realized what she was doing. She quickly picked out her favorite from the photos and sent it to both Cooper and Jacob. It showed Connor's head bent deep, his entire focus on Matthew cradled in his elbow, one hand lifted, bent knuckles angled to caress their son's cheek.

Jacob immediately sent back a selfie of him and Trent, both of them posed with the back of their wrists to foreheads, pretending to swoon, which made her laugh. Connor looked up and saw the phone in her hands. "Hey," he said, his voice rough and deep. "I love you." From the hallway she heard voices, picking out Nate's amidst what sounded like a crowd. Connor grinned. "The hordes are descending." She wrinkled her nose, and he elaborated. "Mom and Dad, Coop, Marie, Nate, probably some cousins. Jordan for sure. Maybe an assistant coach or two..." His voice trailed off, and he smiled. "I love you, Jaime Thompson." Placing their son in her arms, he settled in beside her, wrapping them both up in his strong hold. "Let the festivities begin."

THANK YOU FOR READING
With My Whole Heart!

In this story, which I'm very pleased you've just finished reading by the way, we were introduced to characters that I fell in love with. Jaime's brother and his better half, Jacob and Trent. Well, they simply wouldn't be quiet, and finally received their own book. I hope you pick up the continuing world in *Bet On Us*, available wherever good books are sold.

books2read.com/betonus

ABOUT THE AUTHOR

Raised in the south, *Wall Street Journal* & *USA TODAY* bestselling author MariaLisa learned about the magic of books at an early age. Every summer, she would spend hours in the local library, devouring books of every genre. Self-described as a book-a-holic, she says "I've always loved to read, but then I discovered writing, and found I adored that, too. For reading...if nothing else is available, I've been known to read the back of the cereal box."

Want sneak peeks into what she's working on, or to chat with other readers about her books? Join the Facebook group! **bit.ly/deMora-FB-group**

deMora's got a spam-free newsletter list she'd love to have you join, too: **bit.ly/mldemora-newsletter**

~~~~~

Also by MariaLisa deMora

Alace Sweets, a dark romantic suspense standalone

A dark thriller, this book is not a light read. Filled with edge-of-your-seat suspense, this intense story commands the reader's attention as it drives towards the explosive ending. Alace Sweets is a vigilante serial killer, with everything that implies and is sure to trip all your triggers. Be ready.

At seventeen, Alace Sweets turned a corner in her life, taking the wrong shortcut home from school.

Resisting the harsh knowledge her attackers will never be made to pay for their actions, Alace takes a stand. Justice must be served, and if fate's scales are out of balance, she's determined to set things right as best she can.

When the laws of men fail, the rules of Alace prevail.

5-Star Reviews for Alace Sweets

"Whatever deep dark trench [deMora] pulled a character like Alace from should be revisited again and often."
~Confessions of a Serial Reader

"deMora has a superb story-line and exceptional character development. All of her characters have such depth that will intrigue the reader..."
~Turning Another Page

"Hot, sweet, dark thriller."
~Beth D

"It will keep you on the edge of your seat and give you chills."
~Escape Reality Book Blog

"Disturbing, haunting, sickly; yet hot, sexy and heart racing!"
~Amanda L

"From the first page [deMora] pulls you into the world she has created and you do not even try to escape..."
~Little Shop of Readers Blog

"A must read for all those dark, gritty romance fans out there."
~Sweet & Spicy Reads

"You will find yourself so drawn into the story that the outside world is blocked out and your locking the doors and turning on all the lights."
~Danena F

"Don't judge me for bonding with a vigilante serial killer, she's more than what she does."
~iScream Books

"MariaLisa DeMora, wordsmith that she is, made this a story of the enlightenment of a woman and finding love in a life where she has had none."
~Kat W

~~~~~

Hard Focus, a criminal thriller standalone

This is an intense page-turner, a gut-punch twist-filled story about a woman who has confidence in herself, believes she's a good judge of character, and has filled her life with people she can trust. She's right, but she's also very, very wrong. Readers will have a time of it trying to decide who to watch closest.

Where do you place your trust when your own instincts betray you?

Connie Rowe is a receptionist at a respected legal firm. She's a little bit sassy, a lotta bit happy, has good friends, and is adored by her neighbors.

Life is good.

She's got a boyfriend she enjoys spending time with. He can be a little intense, but he's got a lot going on in his own life, sorting out his young daughter and nightmare of an ex.

Life is grand.

"Trust your gut." That's what Connie's police officer father told her often, training his daughter to believe in herself through the years.

But … what happens when you can't? When your intuition lies?

What happens when things come into Hard Focus?

5-Star Reviews for Hard Focus

"Hard Focus is one very well-written tale. 5 stars is not enough for me."
~Tabitha

"What a powerful story. [deMora] kept me invested from the first word to the last."
~Jesse R

"[deMora] has a certain magical touch to writing her characters, that they become either your nemesis, your best friend, or your love interest. That is certainly portrayed in this spin around. Loved it, loved it, loved it."
~Sandy K

"I strongly recommend this book for both entertainment and to broaden your knowledge of certain laws that must be revisited."
~Words Turn Me On

"A intense page turner. Once you start, you can't put the book down."
~Tracey H

"A beautifully written, powerful read that I can't rate highly enough. This story will stay with me always."
~Gayle

"This book had twists I didn't see coming. Loved it!"
~Lori R

"Wow! I am in awe of deMora's skill in crafting this story."
~Kat W

"I keep sayin that there just aren't enough stars to give to some of Marialisa deMora's books...this one is no different!"
~deLane

"Where do I start with this one...I read this in 3 1/2 hours uninterrupted, I absolutely could NOT put it down. Very deep, keeps you guessing, what's gonna happen next, kind of book. I love how strong her characters are, especially the females!"
~Wendy I

"Sometimes I feel like MariaLisa deMora is the one I should be watching out for. I started reading her books because I'm addicted to MC Romance, but then she decides to change things up and I just follow her wherever she leads me like a Pied Piper. I never know what to expect, and sometimes I'm afraid to find out, but it's always an adventure."
~Rosa for iScream Books Blog

"A plot full of twists and turns, a story that's not quite what it seems, strong characterization, jaw dropping revelations... what more do you need from a book?"
~Manda M

"This book kept me turning the pages wondering what was going to happen. I am usually pretty good at guessing twists but not with this book. She totally surprised me and brought me out of my funk. 5 stars."
~Glenna M

"What an amazing story! Filled with a smidge of suspense, a dash of action and a heap of realism of our country's laws and how their vague application to victims can adversely affect its citizens and the people in their lives."
~Naughty Mom Story Time

Neither This Nor That MC romance series

Legends are born from moments like these. Folktales spun around a single point in time so perfect, you can almost hear the click resonating through the universe as things align. Meet Twisted, Po'Boy, Retro, and Ragman, good old boys from southern states who have many things in common. First, is a bone-deep love of the biker lifestyle. Second, would be their love of the brotherhood, and knowing that you trust the man at your back. Finally, these men have the love of a good woman. None of these come without a price, and it is our pleasure to journey along with them as they discover the blessings that can be won, and lost along the way.

This is the Route of Twisted Pain
Treading the Traitor's Path: Out Bad
Shelter My Heart
Trapped by Fate on Reckless Roads
Thunderstruck

This is the Route of Twisted Pain
"This is the Route of Twisted Pain is an exhilarating, gripping romance novel contrived of incredible world building, complex yet relatable characters, and a unique, captivating plot.
Gifted storyteller MariaLisa deMora beautifully balances exciting suspense, fast action, intriguing secrets with delicious, blazing hot romance scenes.
Readers will be up all night with this riveting page-turner."
~ NY Literary Magazine

I am completely tickled in my fancy for TWISTED!
First off, let me state that there was one thing I didn't like about this book and that is the LAST PAGE! I hated for it to end. I dearly loved this book and its characters as well as their setting.
~Colleen M.

Gripping tale
Twisted and Penny fit together beautifully. The book covers so much more than just their love story. Great introduction to the Incoherent MC. The tale is gripping and gritty. The journey is full of twists and turns that keep you on the edge of your seat. I couldn't put it down. Cannot wait for the next one.
~Lillmil

Twisted is one of the most original and interesting characters I have read in a long time. Marialisa's character building is setting a high bar for her to follow, she will hopefully continue with Po'Boy's story. The Route of Twisted Pain was pure brilliance, and I highly recommend this read.
~Penny T.

This book obsessed me!
This may be the best book I read all year.
These people...they're not characters, they're real... have stuck in my head from the day I met them.
MariaLisa deMora can throw words down that'll Twist (hehe) your insides up till you can't breathe for waiting to hear what's next!
I'm working my way through her other 'families' and yup....she really is that good.
~DeLane

Treading the Traitor's Path: Out Bad
"Treading the Traitor's Path: Out Bad is a solidly engrossing, well-written novel by a talented author. MariaLisa deMora delivers a thrilling ride filled with exciting suspense, deliciously explicit, vivid sex scenes, and gritty, fast-paced action. Her characters are smart, complex, and strong with sharp edges. The settings meticulously detailed.
Fans of Motorcycle Club romance stories will not want to miss this second installment in deMora's exciting series."
~ NY Literary Magazine

What an amazing read! DeMora does not simply wrote a book, she pulls you into a different world. When you read her work, you are very much surrounded by the characters and setting. Prepare for a book hangover because once you finish the book, you will still be stuck with Po Boy.
~KW

THIS WAS AMAZING. Highly recommend for a good story line, interesting characters. I just wish there was more more more.
~Laura

Loved This Book!
What did I just read?! Is my kindle still working? I'm pretty sure it combusted into flames while reading this story. RED HOT READ for 2017. Not what I was expecting at all! I tend to stay away from ménage a trois, because for me it's hard to say there's any kind of conflict except for jealousy, and the ending kind of leaves things unresolved and unrealistic. NOT THIS BOOK! The best one out there guaranteed.
~Linda A

...seriously this series is just WTF so freaking good. Dark, Twisted, harsh, painful and raw. Po'Boy lives for his club, his brothers and his family, there is nothing he wouldn't do for them.
~Fay

I live and breathe for books like this! Fabulously Naughty!...Wickedly Hot! This is my first book by MariaLisa deMora and it will not be my last. MariaLisa delivered a 5 STAR READ! The plot is filled with action, suspense, romance and tons of hot scenes.
~Jenny F

~~~~~

My Rebel Wayfarers MC and the Neither This Nor That MC series do cross over, along with the Occupy Yourself band books, so readers have a couple of choices. The series can be read independently beginning with RWMC, OYBS, and then NTNT without too many spoilers. There's also a crossover between my RWMC world and Lila Rose's Hawks MC world. Or they can be read intertwined—in chronological order.

Here's the recommended reading order if you want to follow according to timing:

Mica, RWMC #1

A Sweet & Merry Christmas, RWMC #1.5

Slate, RWMC #2

Bear, RWMC #3

Born Into Trouble, OYBS #1

Jase, RWMC #4

Gunny, RWMC #5

Mason, RWMC #6

Hoss, RWMC #7

Gypsy's Lady, RWMC #11.5

Thunderstruck, NTNT #5

Going Down Easy

No Man's Land

Cassie, RWMC #12

~~~~~

ADDITIONAL SERIES AND BOOKS

Please note that books in a series frequently feature characters from additional books within that series. If series books are read out of order, readers will twig to spoilers for the other books, so going back to read the skipped titles won't have the same angsty reveals.

Rebel Wayfarers MC series:

Mica, #1
A Sweet & Merry Christmas, #1.5
Slate, #2
Bear, #3
Jase, #4
Gunny, #5
Mason, #6
Hoss, #7
Harddrive Holidays, #7.5
Duck, #8
Biker Chick Campout, #8.5
Watcher, #9
A Kiss to Keep You, #9.25
Gun Totin' Annie, #9.5
Secret Santa, #9.75
Bones, #10
Gunny's Pups, #10.25
Never Settle, #10.5
Not Even A Mouse, #10.75
Fury, #11
Christmas Doings, #11.25
Gypsy's Lady, #11.5
Cassie, #12
Road Runner's Ride, #12.5

Occupy Yourself band series:

Born Into Trouble, #1
Grace In Motion, #2 (TBD)
What They Say, #3 (TBD)

Neither This, Nor That MC series:

This Is the Route Of Twisted Pain, #1
Treading the Traitor's Path: Out Bad, #2
Shelter My Heart, #3
Trapped by Fate on Reckless Roads, #4
Thunderstruck, #5

Rebel Wayfarers & Incoherent MC (NTNT) crossover stories:

Going Down Easy
No Man's Land

Mayhan Bucklers MC series:

Most Rikki-Tik, #1
Mad Minute, #2
Pucker Factor, #3
Boocoo Dinky Dau, #4 (TBD)

Borderline Freaks MC series:

Service and Sacrifice, #1
More Than Enough, #2
Lack of Inbetween, #3
See You in Valhalla, #4

**If You Could Change One Thing:
Tangled Fates Stories**

There Are Limits, #1
Rules Are Rules, #2
The Gray Zone, #3

Other Books:

With My Whole Heart
Bet On Us
Alace Sweets
Hard Focus
Dirty Bitches MC: Season 3

More information available at **mldemora.com**.